FACES OF DEATH

Suddenly a pebble fell near Touch the Sky's feet.

Had he kicked it loose?

Another pebble, and now fear coated his tongue in a coppery dust, for he had recalled something, a "game" Sis-ki-dee had once played when Touch the Sky had sighted the railroad spur through the San Arcs. The renegade had remained in hiding, tossing pebbles and making rattlesnake sounds to unnerve the Cheyenne, letting him know that he was a mere bug inching along the face of the mountain—a bug he could flick off at any moment.

Just as he could flick him off now again.

Before Touch the Sky could fight down the blind panic caused by his helplessness, a hard wind whipped up and simultaneously pushed the clouds away from the moon while also parting the tendrils of ghostly mist.

Just enough for Touch the Sky to see that he was completely ringed in by a grinning Sis-ki-dee and his well-armed warriors!

The *Cheyenne* Series published by *Leisure Books:*

CHEYENNE

13

WENDIGO
MOUNTAIN
JUDD COLE

LEISURE BOOKS   **NEW YORK CITY**

A LEISURE BOOK®

March 1995

Published by

Dorchester Publishing Co., Inc.
276 Fifth Avenue
New York, NY 10001

Printed in the United States of America.

Prologue

In the year the white man's winter-count called 1840, a Northern Cheyenne warrior was born to face a great but bloody destiny.

His original Cheyenne name was lost forever after a bluecoat ambush near the North Platte killed his father and mother and 30 other Cheyennes riding under a truce flag. The squalling infant was the lone survivor, and his life was spared by the officer in charge. He was taken back to the Wyoming river-bend settlement of Bighorn Falls near Fort Bates. There, he was adopted by John Hanchon and his barren young wife, Sarah.

Owners of the town's thriving mercantile store, the Hanchons named the boy Matthew and loved him as their own son in spite of occasional hostile looks and remarks from other settlers. But their affection couldn't save Matthew when he turned 16 and made the mistake of falling in love with Kristen, daughter of the wealthy and hide-bound rancher Hiram Steele.

Steele had Matthew severely beaten when he caught the Cheyenne youth and Kristen in their secret meeting place. Steele also warned Matthew to stay away from Kristen if he wanted to live. Frightened for Matthew's safety, Kristen lied and told him she never wanted to see him again. Although he was full of hate for the white men who meant to harm him, Matthew loved his parents and Kristen too much to leave Bighorn Falls.

But an arrogant young lieutenant from Fort Bates was also in love with Kristen. He altered Matthew's life forever when he issued an ultimatum: Matthew had to leave Bighorn Falls for good or his parents would lose their lucrative contract with Fort Bates—the backbone of their business.

Thus began the odyssey of the brave but lonely Cheyenne youth trapped between two worlds and welcome in neither. His heart sad but determined, Matthew set out for the upcountry of the Powder River—Cheyenne territory.

He was immediately captured by braves from Chief Yellow Bear's Northern Cheyenne camp. His clothing, manners, and speech marked him as an enemy. Declared a spy for the blue-bloused soldiers, he was tortured and sentenced to die. But just as a young brave named Wolf Who Hunts

Smiling was about to gut him, old Arrow Keeper intervened.

The tribe shaman and protector of the sacred Medicine Arrows, Arrow Keeper had recently experienced an epic vision. His vision foretold that the long-lost son of a great Cheyenne chief would return to his people—and that he would lead them in one last, great victory against their enemies. This youth would be known by the distinctive mark of the warrior, the same birthmark Arrow Keeper spotted buried past the youth's hairline—a mulberry-colored arrowhead.

Keeping all this information to himself to protect the youth from jealous tribal enemies, Arrow Keeper used his influence to spare the prisoner's life. This infuriated two braves, especially the cunning Wolf Who Hunts Smiling and his fierce older cousin, Black Elk.

Black Elk, the tribe's war leader despite his youth, was jealous of the glances cast at the tall young stranger by Honey Eater, daughter of Chief Yellow Bear. And the proudly ambitious Wolf Who Hunts Smiling had turned his heart to stone against all whites without exception. He believed this stranger was only a make-believe Cheyenne who wore white man's shoes, spoke the paleface tongue, and showed his emotions on his face like the woman-hearted white men.

Arrow Keeper buried the youth's white name forever and called him Touch the Sky. But the youth soon found that acceptance did not come as easily as his new name. At first, as he trained to be a warrior, Touch the Sky was humiliated at every turn. And his enemies within the tribe tried relentlessly to prove Touch the Sky was a spy for the whiteskins.

By dint of determination, guts, and the cunning he learned from whites, Touch the Sky not only became the greatest warrior of the *Shaiyena* nation, but also made great progress in the shamanic arts, thanks to Arrow Keeper's training. His fighting skill and courage won him more and more followers, including the ever loyal brave, Little Horse.

But with each victory, his enemies managed to turn appearances against him, to suggest that he still carried the white man's stink, which brought the tribe bad luck and scared off the buffalo. And although the entire tribe knew that Touch the Sky and Honey Eater were desperately in love, Honey Eater was forced into a marriage with Black Elk—who chafed in jealous wrath, plotting revenge against Touch the Sky and the woman.

But most dangerous of all—a graver threat than Pawnees, land-grabbing renegades, whiskey runners, buffalo hiders, Crow Crazy Dogs, mad turncoats, the U. S. Cavalry, and the other enemies he defeated—was the treacherous and ambitious Wolf Who Hunts Smiling. Having formed secret alliances with Comanche and Blackfoot renegades, Wolf Who Hunts Smiling planned to raise the lance of leadership over the entire Cheyenne nation and lead a war of extermination against the whiteskin settlers. Only one obstacle prevented his final bid for absolute power: the tall brave named Touch the Sky.

Chapter One

Early in the Moon When the Green Grass Is Up, Touch the Sky rode out with other braves to hunt for antelope in the valley of the Little Bighorn. The hunters returned in five sleeps, their travois piled high with fresh meat. But even as the hunting party crested the last rise before reaching camp, Touch the Sky's shaman sense pricked at him like a cactus spike, warning of new trouble.

Their Sister the Sun had gone to her resting place, and Uncle Moon owned the sky. Touch the Sky spotted Gray Thunder's summer camp the moment they topped the long rise. The village was located in the lush grass where the Powder River joined the Little Powder west of the Black Hills.

Even from there, he could hear the crier racing

10

up and down through the camp, announcing their arrival. Touch the Sky's muscles felt heavy and tired from the journey and the arduous hunt. It would be good to bathe and sleep. Yet as he glanced below at the welcome and familiar sight, something again seemed amiss. But what?

The tipis were erected in their ancient clan circles, all with their openings pointed toward the rising sun, the source of all life. The hide covers had become parchment-thin as they'd aged, and the tipis looked like glowing orange cones because they had fires burning within.

As he rode down following River of Winds, Touch the Sky's eyes automatically sought out the biggest and finest tipi in camp, one with bead-inlaid entrance flaps and several meat racks out back. Spotting the elongated shadows of Black Elk and Honey Eater, he glanced quickly away again, his heart racing.

Thinking of Honey Eater trapped in that tipi with the fierce and jealous Black Elk made Touch the Sky forget whatever had bothered him upon spotting the camp. He fell into a gloomy reverie as the hunters left the meat in the care of Tangle Hair. A Bowstring soldier respected for his honesty, he would distribute it in equal piles to the clan leaders.

"Little brother!" Touch the Sky called out, spotting a youth of 16 winters named Two Twists. "Where is Little Horse?"

"You will see him soon enough," Two Twists replied evasively, hurrying away.

This odd behavior made a deep furrow appear between Touch the Sky's eyes. Two Twists admired him greatly. Why would the young brave suddenly avoid him like this? Clearly, there was something he was afraid to tell him.

Touch the Sky rubbed his pony down with sweet grass and turned her loose in the common corral, then crossed to his own tipi. Since he belonged to no clan in Gray Thunder's tribe, his tipi stood by itself on a lone hummock near the river. He paused beside the light of a huge fire and stooped to borrow a piece of glowing punk. The lurid orange reflection limned his sharply defined features. He was lean, straight, and tall, with a strong hawk nose and piercing black eyes. His hair fell in long, loose locks, cut short over his brow to keep his vision clear. He wore beaded leggings, a doeskin breechclout, and elkskin moccasins. He also had a wide leather band around his left wrist for protection from the sharp slap of his bowstring.

Touch the Sky threw back the hide flap over his tipi entrance, using the glowing punk to ignite the shredded bark kindling in his firepit. The bigger sticks soon flamed to life and shot orange spear tips up, pushing the shadows back. Then he glanced down and saw atop the heap of his sleeping robes a pictograph message made with claybank war paint on a flap of doeskin. Puzzled, Touch the Sky at first paid only scant attention to the series of crude illustrations: a lone mountain peak shrouded in clouds, an eagle tail feather, what appeared to be an underground tunnel. He was more concerned with figuring out who had left it there—a friend or a foe.

The message must have something to do, he decided, with Two Twists's odd behavior. And perhaps with that nagging premonition Touch the Sky had felt when nearing camp.

If anyone in camp knew about this, he thought as he left his tipi and started across the camp clearing, Arrow Keeper would be the one. Although Touch the Sky had barely 20 winters behind him, he knew that a man was not wise simply because he was old. There were plenty of old fools among the red men. But Arrow Keeper was undoubtedly a wise Indian. Age had not dulled the vital spark in his eyes or his dagger-sharp insight into the human heart. As a shaman, he had medicine that was respected from the banks of the Powder River to the Land Beyond the Sun. He had been the tall youth's first friend in the red man's world, and it had been he who had initiated Touch the Sky in the survival secrets of the warrior and in the esoteric arts of the shaman. Many times his help had pulled Touch the Sky back from the jaws of death.

Touch the Sky glanced ahead, then pulled up short in confusion. The hummock upon which Arrow Keeper's tipi had always stood was empty! Instead of the familiar tipi with its cooking tripod out front, Little Horse waited for him.

"How was the hunt, brother?" his sturdy little friend greeted him, handing Touch the Sky a loaded clay pipe.

Despite his agitation, Touch the Sky knew the custom. Clearly, Little Horse had something important to tell him, something much too important to broach immediately. So they sat upon the ground and smoked for a time, speaking of inconsequential matters. Finally Little Horse laid the pipe down between them, the signal that he was ready to speak.

"Brother," he said solemnly, "I have a thing for you."

Every important transition in Indian life was marked by the giving of a gift. Little Horse handed Touch the Sky something small, hard, and highly polished. Touch the Sky leaned into a shaft of silver moonlight to examine it.

"Why, it is Arrow Keeper's magic bloodstone! He told me once that it made his tracks invisible to his enemies. Then, has he. . . . Is he—"

"Brother, every warrior in this tribe would have cropped his hair short in mourning if Arrow Keeper had crossed over to the Land of Ghosts. Be easy. We may yet speak his name aloud without fear his ghost will answer. He is alive."

"Then, buck, where is he? Where is his tipi?"

"He left. As for his tipi, he said in good time it will become his death wickiup."

"Brother," Touch the Sky protested, frustration creeping into his tone, "this is no time to speak like a peyote soldier. You say I may still pronounce Arrow Keeper's name, but then you speak of his death wickiup. Where is our tribe's shaman and Keeper of the Arrows?"

"I am looking at him, buck."

Touch the Sky shook his head impatiently. "The whole world knows I am only Arrow Keeper's assistant. I would need twenty more winters behind me to even dream of attaining his medicine."

"I have no ears for this. And neither does Arrow Keeper. He told me to tell you this thing. His magic bloodstone—do you understand that it was his prized possession? It is yours now because you are the tribe's shaman. And buck, I have the Sacred Arrows. I am holding them for you."

This last pronouncement left Touch the Sky speechless with confused wonder. This was all too much, all too sudden. Little Horse spoke again, his voice urgent.

"Pick up these words, Cheyenne, and carry them in your sash always. Arrow Keeper bade me speak them to you. You know that he was ailing, that red speckles had lately appeared in his cough?"

Touch the Sky nodded.

"Just before you rode out for the hunt, Arrow Keeper decided he had to leave to build his death wickiup and make his preparations for the Last Path while he still had strength to do so. He intended to wait until your return to hold private council with you. But then, he told me, he experienced a powerful medicine vision, one that foretold new suffering for you—and for Honey Eater."

"Honey Eater?" Touch the Sky cut in sharply. "What manner of suffering for her?"

"I know not, buck. Only his words. 'There will be trouble ahead for Touch the Sky, trouble behind for Honey Eater.' That painting you clutch in your hand is a key to Arrow Keeper's vision and this new trouble. He said to tell you that, after this vision was placed over his eyes, he realized you must now act on your own or you will never survive the schemes and dangers your enemies have in store for you."

Arrow Keeper gone! Touch the Sky still could not register that brutal fact. Always, when all had seemed lost and Touch the Sky's last breath was in his nostrils, the old shaman had been there with just enough medicine to help the beleaguered young brave defeat his enemies.

"But brother," he said, "how can I safely guard the Medicine Arrows? You know my situation in camp."

Little Horse nodded. "Arrow Keeper spoke of this. He said you have too many enemies to keep the Arrows in your tipi as he did. But you will be the Keeper of the Arrows. No one else has your gift of visions, your strong medicine. No one else can fight harder to protect them. He has selected a temporary hiding place near camp where you must keep them.

"Tonight, even before you visit the sweat lodge and then sleep, you must take the Arrows to their new place. They will be safe enough there until you decide on a permanent spot known only to you."

"I will, certainly. But what have the others said about having White Man Runs Him as their shaman?" Touch the Sky asked, his tone becoming scornful as he used the name Wolf Who Hunts Smiling had given him.

"For now only Chief Gray Thunder knows. Though Gray Thunder plays no favorites, he has grown to admire you. This will be discussed at the next Council of Forty."

"Expect a lively council, buck! Now let us go get the Arrows from your tipi while you tell me their new hiding place."

Dark clouds blew in from the west, and the breeze grew cooler as a threat of rain filled the night air. Thunder rumbled and bone-white tines of lightning danced on the horizon. From behind a thick deadfall, Wolf Who Hunts Smiling and Medicine Flute silently spied on Touch the Sky.

Periodic lightning flashes illuminated the young warrior clearly. He knelt in the middle of a small willow copse located beyond the first bend in the Powder north of camp. A flat rock shaped like a box lid had been lifted away from a neatly dug hole beneath it. Now the two spies watched Touch the Sky lift out a piece of bright yellow oilcloth.

He spread open the weatherproof cloth, then carefully laid a coyote-fur pouch inside it and wrapped it tightly. Wolf Who Hunts Smiling knew full well that inside that pouch lay no less than the very fate of the tribe: four stone-tipped arrows, their shafts dyed bright blue and yellow and fletched with scarlet feathers—the sacred Medicine Arrows.

"Did I not tell you we need only watch him close?" Wolf Who Hunts Smiling gloated in a whisper. "Now the future belongs to us, shaman!"

Wolf Who Hunts Smiling had been aptly named. He was a compact, powerful buck slightly younger than Touch the Sky. His furtive sneer was matched by swift-as-minnow eyes that darted everywhere at once, always watching for the ever expected attack.

In contrast, Medicine Flute watched Touch the Sky from indolent, heavy-lidded eyes. He was the only brave in camp who had challenged Touch the Sky's claim to the title of shaman. Slender, lazy, and untested as a warrior, Medicine Flute was named after the human-bone flute upon which he constantly piped his eerie, toneless notes.

While still young, the intelligent and perceptive youth had realized that visionaries were highly respected by red men, that they did not have to hunt and fight and work as other braves did. So he pretended to have visions and eventually convinced most of his clan that he possessed medicine. With Wolf Who Hunts Smiling goading him on, he had once awed the entire tribe by performing a miracle: setting a star on fire and sending it blazing across the heavens.

But in fact, Wolf Who Hunts Smiling had talked to a reservation Indian educated in a whiteskin school. This so-called miracle was really a comet, and the whiteskin shamans had predicted its passage. Nonetheless, Medicine Flute claimed credit for the spectacular celestial demonstration, which had struck many in the tribe dumb with awe. Wolf Who Hunts Smiling had ambitions to set Medicine Flute up as tribal shaman, thus wresting control of the tribe from Touch the Sky and his allies.

"But, brother," Medicine Flute objected now in a whisper, "surely you do not intend to harm the Arrows?"

"Harm them, buck? Of course not. But we will use them to send a white man's dog to his funeral scaffold."

Despite their nefarious schemes and lack of faith in most of the Cheyenne spirit lore, neither brave was so blasphemous as to actually harm the four sacred Medicine Arrows. Every Cheyenne was taught from birth that the fate of the Arrows was the fate of the tribe. It was the Keeper of the Arrows' solemn duty to protect them with his life, to keep them forever sweet and clean. Once, a Pawnee band had stolen the Sacred Arrows. Until the tribe had managed to retrieve them, every sort of ill luck and tragedy befell the Cheyennes.

"But if we are not going to harm them," Medicine Flute said, "what is left? Surely you are not so soft-brained as to steal them?"

"Steal them is exactly what I intend to do."

Medicine Flute's heavy-lidded eyes shot open wide. "Brother, have you been struck by lightning? The Council of Forty will feed our livers to the camp dogs if they catch us with the Arrows!"

"We will not have them, buck. Rest easy on that score."

"Who will?"

Another flash of lightning revealed the lone brave in the clearing as he pulled the flat rock back into place. It fit naturally under a thick bush of nettles, safe from animals and curious humans. That same lightning flash revealed Wolf Who Hunts Smiling's lupine grin and hateful, scheming eyes.

He gazed off toward a dark and indistinct mass on the horizon—the rugged Sans Arc Mountains. One peak rose high into the night sky. Fine threads of lightning wrapped the craggy summit like a nest of writhing snakes. Again Wolf Who Hunts Smiling thought about the Blackfoot Indian word-bringer who had recently searched him out with a message.

"You will soon meet the brave who will hold the Arrows," Wolf Who Hunts Smiling promised. "The same brave who is finally going to help us send White Man Runs Him to sleep with the worms."

Chapter Two

"Of course I know what they are," said the Blackfoot renegade named Sis-ki-dee, gazing down at the Medicine Arrows. "You Cheyennes have many foolish beliefs. If I started to piss on them right now, both of you superstitious warriors would try to kill me."

Sis-ki-dee threw back his head and roared with laughter when he saw how nervous his comments made the two Cheyenne visitors. He had no patience for supernatural foolishness. Men kept their weapons to hand and feared no god but the gun. But this wily Wolf Who Hunts Smiling, Sis-ki-dee reminded himself, was a useful ally. Best to humor him and his canny-looking companion, Medicine Flute.

He spoke in the odd mixture of Sioux and

Cheyenne used as a lingua franca among Plains Indians. "No need to pale, bucks! Foolish or not, your magic Arrows are safe with me. We must all cooperate to flush out our quarry and close the net on him—this tall brave they call the Ghost Warrior and the Bear Caller."

"Ghost Warrior!" Wolf Who Hunts Smiling spat into the fire to show his contempt. "He is merely clever at deft tricks mistaken for magic. No one in my camp, except his constant shadow Little Horse, claims to have seen this great battle up north where Touch the Sky turned Bluecoat bullets to sand. I call him Woman Face and White Man Runs Him."

"He is called many things—behind his back," Sis-ki-dee remarked quietly in his own language to his lieutenant, Takes His Share, who sat beside him.

Sis-ki-dee commanded a band of 30 battle-hardened warriors. The number had been closer to 50 until his first encounter with the tall Cheyenne. That had been in these same Sans Arc Mountains, when Sis-ki-dee had attempted to exact tribute from the whiteskin miners who were building a railroad spur. Unfortunately for Sis-ki-dee, Touch the Sky had served as the miners' pathfinder—and left the mountains strewn with dead Blackfoot warriors.

The four braves were holding council near the craggy summit of Wendigo Mountain. The highest peak in the Sans Arc range, it was also considered a tabu spot by most Plains Indians—

the very reason Sis-ki-dee had chosen it for his defensive bastion. Wendigo Mountain was steep and virtually unscalable. It had been scoured by wind and rain for millennia until it was worn down to sheer cliffs except for one narrow, talus-strewn approach. The Cheyennes had ridden up that approach to get here. The camp was further protected by sentry outposts, natural obstacles, and man-made pitfall traps.

The Blackfoot looked at Wolf Who Hunts Smiling, his eyes aglitter with the sickness in his soul. Also called the Contrary Warrior and the Red Peril, Sis-ki-dee had once roamed the rugged country around the Bear Paw Mountains in the northern Montana Territory. But his ruthless, murdering attacks on immigrant trains and bullwhackers had earned a high bounty on his scalp and sent him fleeing south to the Sioux-Cheyenne ranges.

"This plan of yours. I agree it might work."

"It *will* work, Contrary Warrior. The old shaman, Arrow Keeper, has finally dragged his rotting carcass off to die. Now the Council of Forty must decide who will be my tribe's new shaman and Keeper of the Arrows. It will come down to only two choices, the only two braves in the tribe said to possess medicine: White Man Runs Him and Medicine Flute here."

Sis-ki-dee grinned. Big brass rings dangled from slits in his ears, and heavy copper brassards protected his upper arms from enemy lances and arrows. His face was badly marred by smallpox scars. In defiance of the long-haired tribe that had banished him forever, he and all of his contrary braves wore their hair cropped ragged and short.

"You," he said to Medicine Flute. "Do you believe in medicine too?"

"Dangle all the red man's medicine from an empty coup stick," the young brave replied, "and you still have an empty coup stick."

Sis-ki-dee approved this with another grin and a crazy-brave glint to his eyes.

"Unfortunately," Wolf Who Hunts Smiling resumed, "White Man Runs Him will almost surely be selected. Sentiment for old Arrow Keeper runs high among the elders, and this Touch the Sky was the doting old fool's favorite. Yet if I am to take command of the people, I must have my own shaman in power. That means White Man Runs Him must be killed. My ransom plan will accomplish this thing. Then, Contrary Warrior, we two will command a red empire between us."

Sis-ki-dee risked a swift exchange of ironic glances with Takes His Share. We two indeed that glance said. Sis-ki-dee shared power with no one. And the cunning sheen to Wolf Who Hunts Smiling's eyes said that he, too, was not one for dividing up an empire. This was the way the insane Sis-ki-dee liked things to be: treacherous and dangerous, with worthy enemies locking horns in a bloody fight to the death.

But more than anything else, he wanted this tall Cheyenne sent over forever. He had once, in front of the Contrary Warrior's entire band, defeated Sis-ki-dee in a Blackfoot Death Hug: a knife fight with the two opponents' free arms bound together at the wrists. Not only did Touch the Sky win the fight, he humiliated Sis-ki-dee by knocking him out but not killing him—saying, in effect, that he was on a level with soft-brains and women, not worthy of killing.

And that had been a serious mistake. For it was always better to kill a man outright than to humiliate him, to leave him alive to seek revenge.

"We both want this Ghost Warrior killed," Sis-ki-dee said. "He deprived me of a generous peace price from the whiteskin miners. And you say he was the cause of your being stripped of your coup feathers. But medicine or not, he is a warrior who fights like ten men."

"You speak straight-arrow," Wolf Who Hunts Smiling said. "I have raised my battle axe against him for life. May that white man's dog die of the yellow vomit. But I am the first to say it, he stands behind no warrior when the battle cry sounds. My plan is good, yes. But be prepared for a bloody fight, Contrary Warrior. He will not forfeit his life—nor those Arrows—cheaply."

Sis-ki-dee glanced around at his mountain bastion. Huge boulders provided excellent natural breastworks. A fresh deer carcass hung high in a tree, protected from predators. There were also plenty of stores of dried venison and jerked buffalo. Well-armed braves lounged in small groups before their curved wickiups, drinking

40-rod whiskey and gambling with stones. He glanced further up, toward the very pinnacle of the mountain. Should all else fail, there was a secret escape route known only to him.

A smile creased his scarred face. "Not cheaply, perhaps. But count upon it, buck. He will forfeit his life."

"But not the Arrows," Wolf Who Hunts Smiling reminded his secret ally. "They must be returned after his death."

Sis-ki-dee chanced another sly glance at Takes His Share.

"Of course," he reassured his two visitors. "No harm will come to your Sacred Arrows."

Touch the Sky was working his pony in the common corral when he and Little Horse heard the camp crier announce the arrival of a word-bringer.

News was always an important occasion. The two young braves turned their ponies loose and stepped under the buffalo-hair ropes forming the corral. They joined two of their friends, Tangle Hair and Shoots the Bear. Both belonged to the Bowstring Soldier troop, one of several Cheyenne military societies responsible for enforcing the ancient Hunt Law during the annual buffalo hunts. Together, the four braves headed toward the hide-covered council lodge at the center of camp.

Touch the Sky felt Little Horse watching him closely. No doubt he could see clearly that his friend looked distracted, lost in some private worry.

"You have shed much brain sweat lately, brother. Have you been studying Arrow Keeper's painting?" Little Horse said.

Hearing the old shaman's name quickened Touch the Sky's sense of sadness—and hopelessness. Arrow Keeper was gone, probably forever.

"I have, Cheyenne, and done little else. But I might do better to cut sign in the clouds. I cannot even guess what manner of trouble is headed my way."

He didn't add what really cankered at him: Nor what manner of trouble is headed Honey Eater's way. But as if timed to coincide with this thought, he spotted Honey Eater walking with her aunt, Sharp Nosed Woman.

Her jealous mate Black Elk was nowhere in sight. Taking a chance, the two of them exchanged a long glance, their eyes thirsty to drink each other in. Once more Honey Eater's startling beauty caused a sharp pang in his heart.

Her skin was the shade of flawless topaz, her cheekbones delicately and perfectly sculpted. She wore a pretty blue calico dress, made with cloth from the annual treaty goods Touch the Sky had earned for the tribe when he served as pathfinder for the white miners' spur track. The soft material molded itself to her breasts, to the long, sweeping curve of her hips. She had adorned it with elk's teeth, painted shells, and dyed feathers. Honey Eater had also braided her long hair with fresh white columbine petals.

Quickly, almost in an eyeblink, Honey Eater crossed her wrists over her heart. This was Cheyenne sign talk for love.

"Buck," Little Horse warned him quietly. "This is no time to dream. Black Elk has eyes everywhere."

Touch the Sky spotted Lone Bear, leader of Black Elk's Bull Whip Soldier troop, walking with several of Black Elk's troop brothers. They were watching him closely. Quickly he cast his eyes away from Honey Eater.

"Brothers," Tangle Hair said, staring ahead, "which tribe sent this strange messenger? I can tell any tribe by its style of hair. But never have I seen Indians wear their hair like this."

Touch the Sky and Little Horse spotted the word-bringer at the same time, sitting his buckskin pony in front of the council lodge. His face was set in defiant scorn. Immediately recognizing his raggedly cropped hair, they exchanged a wordless glance. They alone of Gray Thunder's tribe had faced these fierce renegade Blackfoot marauders. Now they knew that, true to his promise, the Contrary Warrior had returned to terrorize their homeland.

Sis-ki-dee's words drifted back to Touch the Sky now from the hinterland of memory, his final words after Touch the Sky had defeated him. *You have won the day, Noble Red Man. But Sis-ki-dee swears this. His trail will cross yours soon enough. And then I will skin your face off and lay it over mine with you still alive to see it!*

Now Touch the Sky at least knew the source of this new trouble Arrow Keeper had foretold. He also spotted Black Elk among the warriors ringing the word-bringer. The Blackfoot rode under a white truce flag. But Black Elk was the tribe's battle leader, a fierce warrior who never trusted a potential enemy inside camp.

Black Elk's younger cousin Wolf Who Hunts Smiling stood nearby, his rifle aimed at the messenger. Both braves darted hateful glances at Touch the Sky as he edged closer. Black Elk's scowl was made even fiercer by the wrinkled, leathery flap of his dead ear, which had been severed by a Bluecoat saber. Black Elk had killed the soldier, then calmly sewn the ear back on himself with buckskin thread.

The word-bringer waited until Chief Gray Thunder emerged from his tipi. His refusal to pay homage to a chief or dismount and smoke to the four directions made it clear that these were not friendly tidings. But by strict Plains Indian custom, no word-bringer—not even an ill-behaved enemy—was ever insulted or harmed.

"Cheyenne people!" he announced. "I have been sent by my war chief, Sis-ki-dee, the Contrary Warrior. Attend well to my words, for they are his words and therefore important."

Touch the Sky watched Black Elk's contemptuous scowl deepen. Who was this arrogant Sis-ki-dee? Only Chief Gray Thunder's curt glance convinced him to remain silent. But Touch the Sky noticed that Wolf Who Hunts Smiling had registered no surprise at hearing the renegade's name. He felt the danger-net tightening, for Touch the Sky knew these two treacherous schemers were secret allies.

"Whatever words you have for my people," Gray Thunder replied, "I have ears to hear. There they stand, attending you. Speak them."

"Cheyenne people, know this. You are now a tribe with a new God. For my leader, the Red Peril of the North, the Contrary Warrior named Sis-ki-dee, has your sacred Medicine Arrows!"

These unexpected words landed on the people with the force of buckshot. Numb shock, then a collective gasp of disbelief, ran through the crowd.

"Look to your Keeper of the Arrows," the messenger added, "and ask him if this is not so."

Everyone in Gray Thunder's camp knew Arrow Keeper had left, that Touch the Sky, as his assistant, would be in charge of the Arrows. Now every face turned to stare at him.

Touch the Sky felt warm blood rush into his face. In that moment his eyes flew straight to those of Wolf Who Hunts Smilings'—and the cruel betrayal in the latter's mocking eyes was as clear as a blood spoor in new snow.

Could he? thought Touch the Sky. Could this ambitious monster have done the unthinkable? Not only sullied the Sacred Arrows, but actually have played the turncoat and given them to an enemy?

"Prove this thing is so," Touch the Sky demanded of the word-bringer.

"Prove it is *not* so," the messenger taunted. "Produce the Arrows."

"Do you take us for a camp of soft-brains? I should remove them from hiding now in front of enemies?"

"Never mind then, buck. You may confirm the truth of it when you will. For now, look on this."

Another collective gasp passed through the crowded clearing when the Blackfoot word-bringer stabbed one hand into the pouched front of his clout and produced a piece of soft coyote fur. It was dyed in the intricate geometric patterns of Gray Thunder's band, distinguishing it from the nine other Cheyenne bands that also possessed a set of Medicine Arrows. Everyone instantly recognized it as the cloth used to wrap the Arrows.

"You traitorous dog!" Black Elk roared, closing on Touch the Sky. "You have ruined your tribe! Now I swear by the four directions I'll send your soul west for good!"

But Chief Gray Thunder, a vigorous and stout warrior though well past his fortieth winter, caught Black Elk's arm before the bone-handled knife could leave its sheath.

"Hold, buck! Do not wade in further until we have looked for snakes."

"Father, there stands the snake. Do you realize what this turncoat has done?"

"I realize what he *appears* to have done. I swear it now by the sun and the earth I live on, and this place hears me: If Touch the Sky has indeed let our Arrows into enemy hands, he has no place to hide from Cheyenne justice.

"But place my words in your sash, Black Elk and any others whose thoughts now run to blood. My first duty is to save those Arrows if Maiyun the Good Supernatural will grant it. Now hold, all of you, until we have some sign to guide our way."

The chief looked at the word-bringer again.

"Your leader did not send you merely to taunt us. We are red men, not slyly bargaining Mexicans who come at a price by indirection. Speak like a man and state your leader's terms for the return of the Arrows."

"The mighty Cheyenne demands plain talk? Very well. Here are words you may pick up and examine. Your tribe claims the fate of your Arrows is the fate of the tribe. Within four sleeps your sacred Medicine Arrows will be bloodied, then burned to ashes, unless a ransom is left where Sis-ki-dee tells you to leave it."

His words stunned the tribe into utter silence. Only Gray Thunder spoke, his voice steady but clearly apprehensive.

"What ransom, buck?"

The messenger's face divided in a wide grin as he whirled his pony to point at Touch the Sky.

"Within four sleeps. And only one price will get them back. The severed head of that tall buck!"

Chapter Three

Takes His Share was still half asleep when a sharp kick to his thigh instantly cleared the cobwebs from his eyes. In a heartbeat he sat up in his sleeping robes, a big-bore Lancaster rifle at the ready.

"Wiser to shoot at the Wendigo than at Sis-ki-dee," his leader greeted him, adding his crazy-brave laughter. "Bring a bloody portion of that deer meat over there and follow me."

The sun had barely begun to rim the eastern horizon, but Sis-ki-dee, whose men swore he never slept, was wide awake and keen for sport. His .44 caliber North and Savage rifle, sheathed in buckskin, protruded from under his left arm.

Takes His Share had learned never to question his insane master. He obediently crossed to a cedar brake just beneath their camp and untied a rope made of braided human hair, lowering the deer carcass and using his twine-handled knife to slice off a hind quarter.

"Time is a bird, stout buck," Sis-ki-dee said as the two braves ascended on foot toward the granite peak of Wendigo Mountain. "And now that bird is on the wing. Four sleeps, and the tall Ghost Warrior's head will roast in our campfire until his brains bubble. Four sleeps, if I play the fox well, and *these*—" (he raised the oilskin-wrapped bundle in his hands) "—will be nothing but a thing of smoke, a memory smell. We will have our ransom *and* the pleasure of destroying these pretty-painted sticks."

Sis-ki-dee's pocked face was ugly in the new day's light, the crazy sheen already clear in his shrewd eyes. As they picked their way through the loose talus, he glanced back down the mountain. His camp was in a cup-shaped hollow just below. Further down, the eerie wisps of mist that always shrouded this accursed mountain moved and shifted like something sinister and alive.

"Takes His Share, you fought this Ghost Warrior alongside me once before. Tell me, buck. Can he penetrate our camp?"

"If it were any Indian but that one, I would laugh at the very thought. A titmouse could not slip in unobserved. But truly, Contrary Warrior, they say his life is charmed, and I believe it. I believe that one could penetrate to the heart of a Bluecoat fort and steal their Star Chief's wife from her bed without waking either of them."

Sis-ki-dee approved these wise words with a nod. Takes His Share's ability to size up a situation, and his penchant for straight talk, were the reasons the Blackfoot leader kept him close to the heart of his schemes.

"Your thoughts graze in the same direction as mine. This is a warrior to be feared and respected as well as loathed. So I will not keep the Arrows in camp. They must be hidden in a manner and place equal to his cunning. I know just the spot."

Soon, their breathing ragged from exertion, the two renegades reached the furthermost peak of the rugged mountain. From here the Wyoming Territory stretched out to infinity around them, the mountains folding into foothills, then flattening to the broad brown plains. The Yellowstone and Bighorn Rivers formed winding silver threads twisting north toward the land of the Mandan, Hidatsa, and Assiniboin tribes.

"Now, buck," Sis-ki-dee said, pointing to a slight opening in the rocks. "See that place? A mountain lion lives in there, a she-bitch with hungry cubs. She needs red meat to give them rich milk. Tear that meat you have into tender gobbets. Then make a trail from the opening across to that rock spine over there. Once you have done it, look sharp and move quickly away downwind. This bitch is in a fighting fettle to protect her cubs. If she pokes out while you are near the opening, I will send her back inside with a shot."

Takes His Share did as he was ordered. Sis-ki-dee took up a position out of sight behind a massive boulder. Takes His Share scrambled nimbly from rock to rock, leaving bloody pieces of meat. Tawny fur soon filled the opening, then a magnificent mountain lion peeked cautiously out, twitching her nose, sampling the air.

Ravenously, she devoured the meat and moved out after more. When she disappeared behind the rock spine, Sis-ki-dee hurried into the den.

It was actually a huge underground cavern, most of whose entrance had been obliterated by a rockslide. Sis-ki-dee had explored it well when he had selected this tabu mountain for his stronghold. Now he held his rifle close to his chest and squeezed through the narrow entrance.

He ignored the squirming cubs in their bed of leaves and debris near the entrance. The cavern opened up into a vast chamber illuminated from surface shafts above. From the rear of this chamber a series of tunnels led to the backside of Wendigo Mountain. They emerged onto cliffs, but with ropes a man could descend. Sis-ki-dee had stashed many things at the end of the tunnels.

Hurrying so as not to meet the she-bitch mountain lion, Sis-ki-dee stepped into the cool air of one of the tunnels. Then he lay his rifle aside and, seeking out rough hand and footholds, climbed high until he reached the wet, cold limestone at the top of the tunnel. When he could climb no further, he secreted the slicker-wrapped Medicine Arrows inside a narrow fissure.

There, he thought as he climbed down. *Those Arrows are now lost to the world.* He didn't really expect the tall Cheyenne to simply offer his head for the Arrows. He would be coming after them. And Sis-ki-dee planned to be ready. For if he killed this Cheyenne with his own hands, there would be no need to return the Arrows.

Sis-ki-dee had lost face in front of his men when the Cheyenne had defeated him. Now the Cheyenne would literally lose his, for Blackfoot warriors often skinned their enemies' faces off instead of taking scalps. They did it while the victim was still alive, and then laid the bloody facial skin over their own, the tormentor's mocking eyes staring at the victim through his own eyeholes.

Grinning his crazy-by-thunder grin, Sis-ki-dee slipped back outside just in time to avoid the returning mountain lion.

"Fathers! Brothers! Have ears for my words, for you know I speak only the straight talk."

The council lodge fell silent when Black Elk stood and spoke these words. He was their war leader and sat behind few men in council. This important emergency meeting of the Council of Forty had been called the morning after Sis-ki-dee's word-bringer announced the ransoming of their Sacred Arrows.

Touch the Sky recalled the joy that had swept

through the ranks of his tribal enemies at the word-bringer's chilling pronouncement. That same sneer of celebration lighted Black Elk's stern face as he spoke.

"You know me well," Black Elk said. "My lips have touched the common pipe we just smoked. I have strewn enemy bones from here to the Marias River, I have counted coup on Apaches, Utes, Pawnees, Crows, and blue-bloused soldiers. When did Black Elk ever hide in his tipi when his brothers were on the warpath?"

Touch the Sky felt the fierce warrior's obsidian eyes search him out as he added:

"Cheyenne bucks! Do you finally see now the results of our foolish indiscretion? Do you finally understand what my cousin, Wolf Who Hunts Smiling, has been warning us all along? Do you finally realize that the well-being of our tribe cannot be entrusted to a white man's dog? Now we are up against it! These are the blackest days our tribe has faced, and there sits the cause of this new woe!"

Touch the Sky felt the hostile glances directed at him. He sorely missed the presence of old Arrow Keeper, always his best and most influential ally in council. But things were not the same as they had been during his early days in the tribe. He also had supporters now in that sea of red faces. Some of them were important supporters.

"This Sis-ki-dee," Black Elk continued. "We know not what manner of man he is, nor even where to find him. We cannot even renew the Arrows as preparation for fighting him. He has the Arrows, thanks to this one."

Now Wolf Who Hunts Smiling rose.

"Fathers and brothers, have ears! I have no desire to speak in a wolf bark against old Arrow Keeper. But everyone knows he grew soft-brained in his frosted years and doted on this Touch the Sky. Otherwise the sacred Arrows would never have been entrusted to him. They should have been left with Medicine Flute, whose big medicine was witnessed by all in the tribe when he set a star on fire. What has this one ever done except lay claims to 'visions' no one but he has seen?"

This was greeted with many approving murmurs. Chief Gray Thunder, presiding over this council of the clan Headmen, folded his arms until it had quieted down.

Now Little Horse rose. Everyone paid attention, even his enemies, for here was a brave honored in council for his fighting courage when he had only 15 winters behind him.

"I have no ears for this! Everyone knows that Black Elk, Wolf Who Hunts Smiling, and many in their Bull Whip Soldier troop have turned their hearts to stone toward Touch the Sky.

"Black Elk, consumed with jealousy, claims that Touch the Sky wishes to put on the old moccasin by bulling his squaw. Wolf Who Hunts Smiling claims Touch the Sky is a spy for the *Mah-ish-ta-schee-da.*"

Little Horse had used the Cheyenne word meaning Yellow Eyes, the name his tribe had given to white men because the first palefaces they ever saw were mountain men suffering from severe jaundice.

"Both of his accusers are warriors to be reckoned with. Indeed, Black Elk trained me and Touch the Sky in the combat arts. But neither brave has truth firmly by the tail. Arrow Keeper is no fool. His medicine is respected throughout the Red Nation. If *he* selected Touch the Sky to be Keeper of the Arrows, then count upon it, the best brave was picked."

Arrow Keeper had many friends in the tribe. This speech, too, was greeted with approving murmurs.

Again Chief Gray Thunder folded his arms until the lodge grew quiet. He looked frustrated. His tribe faced a crisis unprecedented since Pawnees had stolen those same Arrows. Yet this bitter, acrimonious meeting was doing nothing to get the Arrows back.

And get them back Gray Thunder knew they must. The Medicine Arrows were the great flywheel that regulated Cheyenne moral life. An angry brave considering the murder of another Cheyenne, for example, knew that such a crime would also bloody the Arrows, and thus the entire tribe. It was the thought of the Arrows that held most troublemakers in check. Without them, lawlessness might soon descend on the tribe.

"Brothers! I speak as your Chief. The duty of

a chief is not to take one side against the other within his tribe. Rather he must determine the collective will of his people.

"This is what I propose now—that we give over this useless trading of accusations until this emergency is behind us. In good time we will have a special council to select our new shaman and Arrow Keeper. Certainly this is important. But for now, bucks, only think! Four sleeps, and then our fate may be horribly sealed. First things first. For now, our every word, thought, and deed must be aimed at saving those Arrows."

These wise words drew approval from all assembled. Now Touch the Sky rose. He had carefully selected his words. His eyes searched out Wolf Who Hunts Smiling.

"Fathers and brothers, have ears for my words. Count upon it, there is treachery for our tribe, but I am not the source. However, our chief has spoken, and I agree. There will be time later to deal with traitors. For now, only one question looms. What do we do about our Arrows? Rather, what do *I* do? The tribe cannot mount a large war-party for fear of endangering the Arrows. And truly, traitors or not, I must admit that somehow my carelessness led to the loss of our Medicine Arrows. I might simply do the manly thing and offer my head now. But brothers, I know this mad renegade called Sis-ki-dee. I have fought him, and so has Little Horse. He is no brave to trifle with. I tell you now, and this place hears me: He will not return those Arrows no matter how we try to appease him."

"Notice how convincingly this one argues that his own death would be pointless," Wolf Who Hunts Smiling put in scornfully. "No coward, he!"

"And *you* have walked between Touch the Sky and the campfire," Tangle Hair said angrily, alluding to the Cheyenne way of announcing one's intention to kill another. "Now you seize the first opportunity to see him killed."

Again the lodge erupted in noisy debate. Touch the Sky silenced it.

"As our chief said," he resumed, "this occasion is too urgent for pointless fighting. So hear me well, then take my words away with you and examine them later. I have four sleeps to locate those Arrows. If they are not safely returned to our tribe before the time expires, my enemies can hold their victory dance. For even though I know Sis-ki-dee for a liar, even though I know he will not return those Arrows after my death, yet my head *will* be severed in payment."

Chapter Four

"Black Elk! I would speak with you, cousin."

Wolf Who Hunts Smiling's voice sounded loud and clear outside the raised elkskin entrance flap of the tipi. It was late morning, shortly after the council meeting broke up.

Black Elk glanced up from the whetstone he was using to sharpen his knife. He watched Honey Eater, who was gathering her beadwork into a basket woven of willow stems.

"Your war leader hears you," Black Elk called out to his cousin. Then, to Honey Eater: "Where are you going?" he demanded.

"Where I always go at this time of day with my beadwork. To my aunt Sharp Nosed Woman's tipi."

Her disrespectful and resentful tone sent dark blood into his face.

"I know full well why you go there so often. That way, the spindly colt Two Twists can bring you honeyed messages from your randy buck, White Man Runs Him."

"You call him a spindly colt, yet that did not stop you from ordering your Bull Whip brothers to savagely beat him for befriending me. But as you say," Honey Eater continued coldly, "why should I deny it, for clearly Black Elk knows everything."

Quicker than an eyeblink, the hot rage was on him. Black Elk rose and pinned her by both arms. His nostrils flared wide with his suddenly heavy breathing.

"Only one thing makes me forbear from killing you now," he told her in a low, dangerous voice. "I know that Touch the Sky, your stag-in-rut, is now doomed. I am going to let you live to see his death confirmed. But once he is sent across the Great Divide, defiant daughter of a great chief, you will learn exactly what your 'pride' is worth. For I will kill you with my own hand."

"You *would* kill a woman," she shot back defiantly. "Just know this, bold warrior who threatens those he has sworn to protect. What you do to me is of no consequence. I know not if you are involved in this foul business of stealing our Arrows. I know you are no coward, nor do I think you are a traitor. But I know your evil cousin who is out there right now waiting for you. I know he had a wolf's paw in this business—I see it all over his shrewd face. If Touch the Sky is killed for ransom, then I swear by the four directions I will kill your cousin! And one way or another, I will kill anyone else who was involved."

This was so brazen and astounding that Black Elk forgot to feel anger. He uttered a harsh bark of laughter.

"Woman, have you eaten peyote? True, my cousin is as glad as any man must be to know that this tall dog is finally marked out for death. But he had nothing to do with giving our Arrows to our enemy. Your pretend Cheyenne is the treacherous culprit with that sin on his head."

"Cousin!" Wolf Who Hunts Smiling called impatiently. "Are your moccasins picketed to the ground? I am waiting."

Black Elk stepped outside, his dark eyes snapping sparks.

"Does the calf bellow to the bull? I trained you, buck."

Wolf Who Hunts Smiling bit back a sharp reply. In truth, he no longer feared his older cousin, whom he considered too stupid and loyal to do anything except command a battle—which, admittedly, he did second to no brave. But leading an entire nation of Indians, shaping them to a man's purpose—that required a shrewd brain indeed. For now, though, he needed Black Elk and his fellow Bull Whips with him, not against him.

"You trained me, indeed, and a good job, too. My ghost will never cry for lack of good training. But tell me, cousin, do your meat racks need inspecting?"

This was the signal that he wanted to discuss something in private. They moved out behind Black Elk's tipi.

"Cousin," he gloated when they had moved out of Honey Eater's hearing, "Touch the Sky can make the he-bear talk in council. But it is all over now except for the dying!"

"Familiar words. But he has outfoxed death before. This Sis-ki-dee, who is he? We know nothing of his mettle. Why should this Blackfoot renegade succeed where legions have failed?"

Wolf Who Hunts Smiling was careful to tread lightly now. Only Medicine Flute knew of his secret connivance with Sis-ki-dee. Black Elk was covered with hard enough bark but respected most of the Spirit Ways. He would never cooperate in a plot to steal the tribe's Sacred Arrows, no matter how much his jealous wrath desired the death of Touch the Sky. And in fact even Wolf Who Hunts Smiling did not want to see those Arrows harmed. He had begun to have second thoughts about trusting Sis-ki-dee.

"As you say," Wolf Who Hunts Smiling agreed. "But cousin, this mystery brave was wily enough to obtain the Arrows. He may well see this thing through."

Honey Eater emerged from the tipi. Watching her cross the clearing, heading to her aunt's tipi, Black Elk felt the heat of his earlier anger returning. His wily younger cousin watched his face closely and saw which way the jealous buck's thoughts drifted.

"Black Elk," he said, "have you noticed how Woman Face's unbelievable carelessness with our Arrows has turned many against him? Many who had merely been indifferent before?"

"Of course. Who could not notice this? I have eyes."

"As you say. And clearly, if this thing goes badly, it would also tell against those who are loyal to him. Little Horse, Tangle Hair, Two Twists, Shoots the Bear—certain others," he added meaningfully, not having to say Honey Eater's name.

"It would, Cheyenne." Black Elk's tone was more curious, less impatient now, for he realized his cousin was homing in on a target.

Wolf Who Hunts Smiling weighed each word carefully. He was taking a chance here. But this was one of his chief skills: Knowing the soft places where he could grab hold of a man.

"If, for example, a number of reliable braves were to come forth and speak a thing. Say, the fact that a certain married Cheyenne woman lifted her dress for him in secret, that they witnessed this thing. Perhaps more than once. Well, then. . . ." Wolf Who Hunts Smiling shrugged one shoulder. "Why, the Star Chamber might well absolve a squaw's husband should he understandably become violent and, in a fit of just rage, somehow punish her. Perhaps even slay her."

A long silence followed as Black Elk mulled over his cousin's hints. In the Cheyenne tongue, the word 'murder' was the same as the word 'putrid,' for the murder of a fellow Cheyenne caused the internal corruption of the individual and the tribe. Thus the murder stigma was strong. Even if a murderer was not banned—for the Cheyennes were loathe to banish their own—he could never again smoke from the common pipe or eat from a common utensil. He could never participate in the Renewal of the Arrows or the Spring Dance or the annual buffalo hunt.

Wolf Who Hunts Smiling was reminding him, however, that if Honey Eater were charged with adultery, especially with such a heinous criminal as Touch the Sky, then the Cheyenne Star Chamber would almost certainly absolve him of the act of wife-slaughter. The braves taking part in this secret court of last resort were known only to Chief Gray Thunder, nor could their judgments be questioned.

Black Elk once more recalled Honey Eater's arrogant tone, and her increasing defiance of him. How much humiliation had her love for Touch the Sky caused Black Elk? How many jokes had been spawned by his failure to get her with whelp? He could have crawled off like a whipped dog when Touch the Sky had saved Honey Eater from her Comanche and Kiowa captors after Black Elk had failed. It would be satisfying indeed to finally feel her delicate neck snap in his grip.

He met his cousin's eye. That look sealed a silent agreement.

"Straight talk, buck. As you say, it would go hard for all who were loyal to one who jeopardized the Arrows. Even for a woman."

There will be trouble ahead for Touch the Sky, trouble behind for Honey Eater.

Arrow Keeper's words set up a ghostly refrain in Touch the Sky's thoughts, goading him to action. But *what* action? His only clue was the crude pictograph warning. Puzzle over it as he might, it was like trying to make out the bottom of a muddy river.

You must now act on your own or you will never survive the schemes and dangers your enemies have in store for you.

Never had he felt so alone in a hostile world. Even during his earliest days with the tribe, even before he had learned that Indians mount their horses from the right side, Arrow Keeper had been there with his loyalty and his magic. Touch the Sky's own shaman sense told him that Arrow Keeper was still alive. But it was useless to look for him when he chose not to be found.

As he studied the pictograph while readying his battle rig to ride out, he held his face impassive in spite of the shame he felt. Yes, the wily Wolf Who Hunts Smiling was involved in this thing. But even so, Touch the Sky knew he had somehow been careless. Now the Medicine Arrows were in enemy hands.

Wendigo Mountain

As the result of some hard and bloody fights to prove his bravery and loyalty, Touch the Sky had earned a growing number of supporters within the tribe. Now only a few would visit him with a loaded pipe or even look him in the eye and nod. True death for an Indian, Arrow Keeper had taught him early, is to be alone forever. Until he returned those Arrows, he was alone. And if he did not do it soon enough, he would be dead.

Death, Touch the Sky told himself as he secured an axe to his pony's rope-rigging, he could accept. He feared it, of course, as any sane man does. But he could face it. However, Arrow Keeper was not one to raise an alarm lightly—and how could Touch the Sky protect Honey Eater once he was sent under?

"Brother!"

Startled, he glanced up. It was Little Horse who called to him. He was accompanied by Tangle Hair and his Bowstring Troop brother Shoots the Bear. Also with them was Two Twists, the young warrior named after his habit of wearing his hair in double braids. All four warriors led ponies rigged for battle.

"When do we ride out?" Little Horse called out boldly. "I am keen for sport, nor do I plan to die in my tipi."

Touch the Sky opened his mouth to protest. But then he knew it would be useless. Each one of these braves would gladly die for him. They had made up their minds to ride out. And truly, he welcomed them. He would not embarrass them with thanks.

"When do we ride out?" Touch the Sky lifted the doeskin flap. "As soon as Arrow Keeper's mysterious art yields a first clue."

His friends hobbled their mounts and gathered round him. Touch the Sky opened the simple claybank painting up in the grass in front of his tipi. Each brave crowded close and studied the crude illustrations: a mountain peak, an eagle's tail feather, a dark, curving line.

"Truly," Little Horse said, glancing at the sawtooth horizon all around them, "there are mountains enough in or near our hunting grounds. Nothing about this painting helps us tell which one."

Two Twists squinted and bent closer to the doeskin. "Why did Arrow Keeper smudge this with charcoal?"

"Where, little brother?"

"Here." Two Twists pointed at a spot about halfway up the painted mountain. Touch the Sky looked closer. He had assumed that that smudged girdle was simply dirt that had got on the painting before it dried. But now he saw that Two Twists was right: It was charcoal. Some of it came off on his finger now as he rubbed it.

Little Horse frowned and glanced northwest, toward the Sans Arc range. His eyes narrowed thoughtfully.

"Maiyun grant that I am wrong," he muttered.

Touch the Sky met his eyes. "Wrong about what, brother?"

"This ring about the mountain. It is halfway up. There is a peak in the Sans Arc range, one you cannot see from here. You were close to it when you sighted the track for the iron horse through the Sans Arc pass. You may have noticed it—mostly steep cliffs and loose talus, and it is constantly shrouded in a ring of mist about halfway up."

Touch the Sky nodded. "As you say. I remember it. I remember I was glad the track ran past it, for it was as treacherous as any I have seen."

"Not merely the slope," Little Horse said grimly. "Have you heard the people talk of Wendigo Mountain?"

A cool feather tickled the tall brave's spine. "I have, though I know little about it."

"I should have thought of it before," Little Horse said, musing out loud. "It is exactly the spot that one as cunning as Sis-ki-dee would pick."

"Bad medicine protects that place," Tangle Hair put in, glancing off toward the northwest. "The Cheyenne, the Lakota, the Arapaho, even the mountain-loving Ute—all avoid this place. It is said that any brave who touches its slope will never leave Wendigo Mountain alive."

"What caused such bad medicine?" Touch the Sky said. "The mountains are a gift from the Day Maker, Maiyun. Only a great evil could taint gifts from the Powerful One."

"Only the greatest," Little Horse agreed. He glanced uncomfortably at the rest. Touch the Sky had not grown up with them, hearing the old stories. Reluctantly, Little Horse untied the chamois pouch hanging from his sash. It contained rich brown tobacco traded from whiteskins. He had been saving it for a special occasion. Now, reluctant to talk about such unholy things without paying tribute to the spirits, he scattered it on the ground. Watching him, Touch the Sky felt another chill.

"It happened after the Pawnees stole our Medicine Arrows," Little Horse explained. "Before we were even children on our fathers' knees. A group of Cheyenne hunters were trapped out on the plains by a huge Crow war party. Crow Crazy Dogs—you know them well, buck."

Touch the Sky nodded grimly. Crow Crazy Dogs were highly feared suicide warriors. Once engaged in an attack, they were sworn to either defeat their enemies or die. Touch the Sky and Little Horse had fought them in a fierce skirmish while serving as voyageurs on land-grabber Wes Munro's keelboat.

"The Cheyennes fled into the Sans Arc range. They selected the peak now known as Wendigo Mountain because it was the most formidable. Because of the mists, they did not realize the opposite side was all cliffs."

"The relentless Crazy Dogs," Shoots the Bear took up the narrative, "locked onto the Cheyennes like hounds on a blood scent. They backed them on to the cliffs. The Cheyennes used all their musket balls and arrows."

"Then," Tangle Hair took over, "rather than give the Crazy Dogs the pleasure of torturing them, the Cheyennes all sang their death song. As one, all twelve hunters locked arms and stepped off the cliffs and were impaled on the basalt turrets far below. The bodies were never recovered."

All five Cheyennes made the cutoff sign, as one did when speaking of the dead.

"They died unnatural deaths after dark," Little Horse said. "Bad deaths. Now all twelve are souls in torment, doomed to haunt Wendigo Mountain. Indeed, some swear you can hear their groans in the moaning of the wind. It would be Sis-ki-dee's nature to pick this place, knowing he is safe from attack there."

Touch the Sky looked at the rest. "I am convinced now, brother, that you have truth firmly by the tail. And so I must attack this Wendigo Mountain, tabu or not. Now are the rest of you still keen for sport?"

Indeed, there was little bravado in their manner now. The same Cheyenne who would ride unflinching straight into a stampeding buffalo herd would flee from an easy fight if he were not correctly painted to please the Holy Ones. Nor would he be called a coward, so great was the belief in matters supernatural.

Abruptly, Little Horse thrust out his lance. After the slightest hesitation, the others, too, laid their lances across his.

"We ride after our Arrows," Little Horse vowed. "My life, my honor, are pledged to them. If I fall, it will be on Blackfoot bones. No matter how hard the battle, no matter if I must face the Wendigo himself, I will not flinch. Our enemies have no place to hide from me!"

One by one, the others added their pledge.

"I am riding with the best," Touch the Sky said simply. "Ipewa. Good."

He grabbed a handful of the calico's mane and swung up onto her back. His eyes dwelled one final time on the jagged granite peaks of the Sans Arc range.

"May the Holy Ones ride with us," he prayed softly, and with that the small war party rode out, singing a battle song.

Chapter Five

The five Cheyennes made good time across their familiar ranges. They crossed the flat tableland near the rivers, then the rolling tall-grass plains. Their mounts were strong from the new grass, and rivers, streams, and runoff rills were plentiful.

Even with the imminent danger they faced, Touch the Sky's senses were alert to the beauty around him. The fertile green river valleys dotted with bright verbena and golden crocuses; the pure, quick-flowing water of the Powder and the Little Bighorn; the Yellowstone, teeming with trout and bluegill; the fathomless blue sky, opening like an infinite dome above them. The Cheyenne spotted distant herds of antelope, their white tails flashing in the sun, while pronghorn sheep grazed in the lush bunchgrass.

Time was critical, so the normal routine based on the rising and setting of the sun and moon was abandoned. They simply rode and camped, rode and camped, sleeping briefly; otherwise they paused only to rest and water the horses. They made simple cold camps, killing no fresh game and subsisting on dried venison and pemmican. Following this dogged schedule, the hardy band reached the foothills of the Sans Arc range within one full sleep.

Good time, Touch the Sky knew, but it also meant that only three sleeps remained until Sis-ki-dee's deadline. It was the deadline for his death, certainly, but Touch the Sky couldn't stop reminding himself even his head would not purchase those Medicine Arrows from a brave as hateful and insane as Sis-ki-dee. Touch the Sky would die *and* the Arrows would somehow be destroyed if that crazy renegade had his way.

And Honey Eater, his death would somehow entail her destruction as well. Truly, thought Touch the Sky, it would go hard for anyone who ever showed him friendship and loyalty, including every brave now riding with him.

"Brothers," Little Horse called back as he debouched from a narrow ravine, "ahead lies Wendigo Mountain."

Even before Touch the Sky caught a first glimpse, Little Horse's muted tone alerted him to the daunting nature of this mission. Together they had faced 200 buffalo hiders armed with

Hawken rifles, been mercilessly tortured aboard Wes Munro's keelboat, fought their way out of a whiskey-trader's fortress. But then they had faced only death; now they faced a *bad* death, the kind that left an Indian's soul crying in the wind for eternity.

Touch the Sky's pony flexed her strong hindquarters, leaping up onto the flat, and the young Cheyenne felt a ball of ice replace his stomach.

The Sans Arc range towered before them, rising above steep headlands and deep gorges scrubbed by white-water rivers. The railroad spur that Touch the Sky had sighted through for Caleb Riley and his crew lay far over on the northern slopes. But Wendigo Mountain itself could not be missed at this distance. Its tall peak disappeared into the low gray belly of clouds—and that eerie belt of mist circled it just beyond the halfway point.

"See?" Shoots the Bear pointed. "Only one slope goes up."

"The rest," said Tangle Hair, "is all worn away to cliffs."

"If our enemy waits up there," Two Twists added, "they are as safe as eagles in their nests."

"They are waiting." Touch the Sky believed this even though they had spotted not one sign so far of Sis-ki-dee's band. He saw this thing with the eye Arrow Keeper had taught him to use, the shaman eye, which read sign even the best scouts missed.

"But eagles die, too," he added. "Two Twists is right. Anyone watching that slope could pick us off as if we were turkeys on a log. It hints at a bloody business, brothers. Though time is scarce, we must make a fast scout all the way around the base of the mountain. Scour every piece of it. If there is any other way up, we must take it."

The rest agreed. They divided into two teams, Touch the Sky and Little Horse setting out to the west, Tangle Hair, Shoots the Bear, and Two Twists circling to the east.

The sun tracked further across the sky, and more valuable time slipped away as the two teams circled the mountain. But an alternate route appeared out of the question. With the exception of that one narrow slope up the southern face, only rugged cliffs were visible. And the base of many of these was rendered inaccessible by massive heaps of scree—fallen and broken rock, some of it on the verge of forming dangerous slides. Touch the Sky felt something else during this quick circuit of Wendigo Mountain: the unmistakable presence of great evil. Not just the evil represented by Sis-ki-dee and his murdering band, which was evil enough for this world. What he felt now, even more strongly, was an evil of place—a sense that bad medicine haunted this mountain, a poison waiting to infect any fool who headed up that steep slope.

"The Contrary Warrior knows his business well," Little Horse complained bitterly.

The preliminary scouting was finished, and all five braves had assembled again beneath the southern slope. By now the sun was low in the west, their shadows long and growing purple behind them.

"Did you see any sign of them up there?" Tangle Hair said. "We did not."

Touch the Sky shook his head.

"Perhaps," Shoots the Bear suggested, hope lifting his tone, "they have no sentries on the slope. Perhaps they feel too secure up there to bother."

Tangle Hair and Two Twists nodded at this, as did Little Horse, but Touch the Sky believed they were wrong. Shoots the Bear, however, was a respected Bow String trooper who had distinguished himself in the fight against the buffalo hiders. A Cheyenne leader did not impose his will on his men—he determined the collective desire of the group. Thus, whatever happened later, they had spoken as one and no individual was blamed.

"We will see about this slope," he agreed. "But first let us see if we can outfox the foxes."

Since this was not to be a battle fought on the open plains, the Cheyennes had brought no remounts—only two packhorses in the event they had dead or wounded to haul out. Working quickly, Touch the Sky borrowed a buckskin shirt and trousers from Tangle Hair and Two Twists. Working out of sight of the slope, he stuffed them well with grass and then tied them to the extra mount. A stuffed, feathered headdress was secured to the sham warrior with rawhide whangs.

"Nothing fearsome at this range," he admitted when the crude Indian was ready. "But perhaps he becomes more dangerous with distance." He slapped the pony's rump and sent her up the slope.

For some time the sturdy little high-country mustang picked its way carefully through the talus, as nimble as a mule. The braves watched anxiously from below, unsure how to interpret this.

"Perhaps our enemy is not up there at all?" Two Twist said.

"He is up there," Little Horse suggested, "but there are no sentries on the slope."

"Unless," Shoots the Bear reminded them, "they have recognized our trick. They may be holding back to lure a real Indian target that bleeds."

Touch the Sky opened his mouth to speak. Suddenly he spotted a bright flash of light above, a flash too powerful to have been the mere glimmer of quartz or mica. A flash he recognized as a mirror signal.

A heartbeat later a rifle shot split the silence. The feathered headdress flew from the mock warrior, dragging grass stuffing with it. The pony shied, crow-hopped sideways as it had been trained to do under fire, then turned and raced back down the slope.

Two Twists ran to catch the pony's hackamore. The rest stared at Touch the Sky. Now the sun was a dull orange ball balanced just above the western horizon.

"What now?" Little Horse said. He nodded at the setting sun. "Your trick may have saved one of us, brother. But only three sleeps remain now, and we have done nothing except make them waste a bullet."

Touch the Sky's mouth formed a grim, determined slit.

"We have done nothing, you speak straight-arrow there. As much as I am loath to do it, buck, I see no other course. Our Cheyenne way forbids fighting after dark. But we have no choice. Any brave who wishes may return to camp now and know he is not a coward. For after Sister Sun goes to her rest, we move up that slope."

"Contrary Warrior," Takes His Share said to his battle chief, "I have noticed a thing. You have hidden the Cheyenne Medicine Arrows well. Even I do not know their exact spot. You handled them with great care, I noticed. Do you believe there is medicine attached to these Arrows?"

The sun had flamed out in a fiery blaze of red glory, and now Wendigo Mountain belonged to the night. Despite the warm days, nights were cool up in these altitudes, especially with the constantly shrieking wind. Legend claimed that the shriek was the death cries of those Cheyenne warriors who had plunged off the cliffs long ago.

Sis-ki-dee flashed his crazy-by-thunder grin in the gathering darkness.

"Believe? Would you ask a hawk if it believes a mouse should not be eaten? Stout buck, if I believed their other-world nonsense, I would have destroyed their 'Sacred Arrows' the moment they filled my hands. It is *their* puny faith that grants value to those pretty sticks, not mine. I play their game to keep that value high."

Ten of Sis-ki-dee's best fighters were positioned behind the rocks flanking the narrow slope. The belt of mist around Wendigo Mountain was in fact steam from underground hot springs. A huge fissure had opened above the springs, and steam constantly escaped. Conflicting wind currents formed the permanent belt. Now it lay just below the Blackfoot position. They had pulled back after realizing how the resourceful Cheyennes had tricked them with the dummy warrior.

The night was dark; a cloud-mottled sky and a weak quarter moon made little illumination. Sis-ki-dee had slid his North and Savage .44 from its sheath and now held it at the ready across the top of a boulder. Takes His Share's big-bore Lancaster rifle lay beside it.

"Go remind the others one more time," Sis-ki-dee said. "They may kill any but the tall Ghost Warrior. He is to be taken alive."

Sis-ki-dee knew Touch the Sky would eventually have to die, of course, and it would be a hard death. He had lost status with his men when this tall Cheyenne had defeated him in the Death Hug match at the railroad camp. Sis-ki-dee's authority was based on fear—his men's fear of his own invincibility. Now, every time he failed anew to kill the Cheyenne, he risked his position of unquestionable authority.

Takes His Share materialized beside him out of the grainy blackness.

"They have all been reminded," he assured his leader. "The tall one will be taken alive."

"Good. Their little ruse earlier with the decoy shows they mean to play children's games with us. But soon enough they will not feel so playful."

Sis-ki-dee's tribe did not waste human scalps as trophies. They had discovered that human-hair ropes remained stronger in rain than buffalo or horse hair. Thus scalps were taken to make ropes. As for war trophies, it was their custom to remove an enemy's entire facial skin.

Just thinking about it made Sis-ki-dee grin like a happy baby. How his men would howl and praise his name when he danced around the fire, that tall Cheyenne's wrinkled visage worn over his own face—his own triumph-gleaming eyes peering through the empty holes!

Chapter Six

Touch the Sky's band made a temporary camp in the foothills, waiting for full darkness to settle over the mountains.

As they prepared for their dangerous ascent, they could still make out the dark, looming presence of Wendigo Mountain. Even here, back in the hills, they could hear the terrible shrieking of those winds up on the slope—winds that raised eerie human cries, cries of pain and desolation, but also cries of warning.

How many wise Indians, Touch the Sky wondered, had heard that warning and heeded it?

Not one brave in this band of five had ever shown the white feather. All had been tested in battle, even young Two Twists, who had only 17 winters behind him. Touch the Sky knew they were warriors, each of them straight grain clear through.

And yet none of them had ever faced such a test as this. They had all grown up believing that Wendigo Mountain was a place of terror, suffering, and death, a place to be avoided at all costs. "If you do not behave," Cheyenne mothers often threatened their children, "I'll send you to Wendigo Mountain." They were up against not only a formidable physical foe, but powerful bad medicine as well.

Little was said as they inspected their weapons. Sand was carefully wiped from crimped cartridges, their animal-tendon bowstrings were tightened and closely scrutinized for frayed spots. Little Horse ran all four revolving barrels of his scattergun around to check the action; Touch the Sky made sure he had a fresh primer cap behind the loading gate of his Sharps.

They had no idea what they might encounter, if or how long they might be pinned down. So they stuffed their parfleches and legging sashes with dried venison and bitterroot, as well as strips of cloth for binding wounds. The slope was hard and littered with plenty of sharp rocks and flints. They took the precaution of stuffing their moccasins with dead grass.

As was the custom, each brave said a brief, silent battle prayer as he touched his personal medicine, which was the totem of his clan. These totems were kept in small rawhide pouches on their clouts. Touch the Sky had no official clan.

But Arrow Keeper had presented him with a set of badger claws—the totem of Chief Running Antelope of the Northern Cheyenne, killed in the year the white man's winter-count called 1840, the year Touch the Sky had been born. Arrow Keeper called this chief Touch the Sky's father, and Touch the Sky had never known Arrow Keeper to speak bent words.

"Brother," Little Horse said curiously, who had seen his friend remove the badger claws and pray over them, "I would ask you a thing."

"I have ears to hear you, buck. Ask this thing."

"Brother, we have saved each other's lives more than once. We fought Bluecoats and whiskey-traders and land-grabbers and Pawnees, fought all of them side by side and then smeared our bodies with their blood. We stood shoulder to shoulder at the Buffalo Battle and sent many white hiders' souls across the Great Divide. So tell me only this.

"You know that I have seen the mark of the warrior buried in your hair. An arrow point so perfect it might have been fashioned by Maiyun the Day Maker. And I recall when the Bull Whips set upon you during the buffalo hunt, beating you after Wolf Who Hunts Smiling played the fox and accused you of violating Hunt Law. You told them your father was a great warrior, greater than any in Gray Thunder's tribe."

Touch the Sky nodded. "Certainly I too recall this. The Bull Whips mocked me for a liar."

"They did. But others did not. You fight like

five men—clearly you descend from a stout warrior's loins! But brother, when you sought your great vision at Medicine Lake, was it revealed to you the part you are meant to play in our tribe's destiny? How much was made known to you?"

Touch the Sky thought for a long time. As he did, he sharpened his obsidian knife and stared out toward the shadow of Wendigo Mountain.

"Much was revealed," he finally answered. "But it was like shadow pictures on snow. The shape of things was there, but not the substance."

If this answer confused him, Little Horse did not show it. He merely nodded, accepting these words.

"Truly, I have heard this about visions and medicine dreams. That they convey great truths, yet little that can be told with words."

"As you say. They are felt more than known."

The Cheyennes' final preparation was to wrap their heads in blankets or buffalo robes. This was to prepare their night vision for the moonless trek up that dangerous slope. An hour spent in total darkness would dilate their pupils so much that objects now hidden to sight would take on linearity and depth.

Little Horse's questions had set Touch the Sky thinking about his harrowing vision quest to Medicine Lake. The voice of Chief Yellow Bear, Honey Eater's dead father, had spoken to him from the Land of Ghosts. He had warned him that great suffering was in store for him before he would ever raise high the lance of leadership.

But that vision—which also hinted at a crimson clash of war for the *Shaiyena* nation—did not tell him whether or not Honey Eater would ever share his tipi. Nor, he thought now as he lay in a burrow of grass with his eyes tightly covered, had it warned of any suffering for Honey Eater.

And yet, according to Arrow Keeper, she too now had a grisly share in his danger. That gnawed at the young brave like sharp incisors, for truly Honey Eater had already suffered enough for his sake, especially unfair abuse from the jealous Black Elk.

All these reminiscences about Arrow Keeper brought the old shaman's wrinkled-as-a-peach-pit face firmly into his mind's eye. The wind rose again, a hollow groan that lifted to a shriek. Touch the Sky felt the fine hairs on his nape stiffening when, suddenly, the image of Arrow Keeper was all at once shrouded in wisps of smoke.

No, he realized. Not smoke. Thin tendrils of steam. For Arrow Keeper sat naked in a steaming sweat lodge. And mysteriously, the old man was vigorously shaking his head no, vigorously waving his young assistant back from something.

A strong hand gripped his arm, and Touch the Sky flinched violently.

"It is time now, brother," Little Horse told him. "Wendigo Mountain is waiting for us."

They muzzled their ponies with sashes and belts, wrapped their hoofs in rawhide to quiet them. Then Touch the Sky made the final inspection of his warriors.

"Shoots the Bear?"

"I have ears, brother."

"Remove your bone choker. If the clouds blow off, it may glint in the moonlight."

He glanced at Two Twists. "Smear more mud on your face, buck. It too will glint."

Now he addressed all of them.

"We ride up single file, using the scree as much as possible for cover. Keep wide intervals in case they have a rockslide planned. No one plays the big Indian. If enemy are sighted, try to avoid the fight. Maiyun has forbidden treading the war path by night. Do not goad His wrath by rashly trying to count coup or draw first blood.

"Our mission is to retrieve those Arrows. So the first step is to get up that mountain and near their camp. Hatred, revenge, glory—none of these matter now. The fate of the Arrows is the fate of the people. Keep a keen eye and a steady hand, and commend your soul to the Good Supernatural.

"May the High Holy Ones go with us."

"May it even be so," the rest intoned when Touch the Sky closed on that line of prayer. With that they hit the slope.

Their sure-footed ponies were well grazed and took the rock-strewn slope easily. Touch the Sky took first turn riding point. His tough little calico was rebellious at first as she fought her muzzle. Then she settled into the steady climb, powerful haunches bunching as the slope narrowed and steepened.

The wind howled and screamed and sometimes died down to an eerie whistle before again rising in a shriek that made Touch the Sky's pony sidestep nervously. There were constant, sudden movements in the corner of his vision. But each time he pointed his rifle, there was nothing out there but the black maw of the night.

He was nerved for action, every muscle like a coiled spring. Now and then a scud of clouds blew away from the moon. Then Touch the Sky would glance back down to see his companions moving up behind him.

He led them around a pinnacle, then down into a hollow. He felt it before he saw it: huge, billowing wisps of warm fog. Then he realized it wasn't fog, but steam escaping from the underground hot springs.

They had reached the necklace of 'mist' that encircled the mountain.

Visibility was abruptly reduced; Touch the Sky could only see a few feet ahead. He pulled back on the calico's hackamore, debating. This ring of billowing steam clouds would have to be traversed if they were to ascend.

But it felt wrong. That familiar numb prickle of warning moved up his spine. And he recalled the brief vision he'd just had of old Arrow Keeper. True, the old shaman had been in a sweat lodge, not here on the mountain. But had he not waved him back from clouds of steam?

Time was critical. But only a fool, he decided, ignored spirit signs.

Touch the Sky dismounted and hobbled his pony's legs. Then he called the rest of his band around him.

"I do not like the feel of it, brothers. Wait here. I will sneak through the steam on foot to see if a trap awaits us."

"You hog all the sport," Little Horse objected. "Let me go. I have the best ears in the tribe."

This was true enough, but on this point Touch the Sky did not yield to debate. After all, it was *his* carelessness that had somehow placed the Arrows in danger.

"I will go, and no further discussion of it will stand. Listen for the owl hoot. If I make it up, I'll signal back for the rest to advance. Someone lead my pony."

Holding his rifle close to his chest, Touch the Sky disappeared into the roiling cloud of steam.

Between the steam and the new-tar darkness of the night, Touch the Sky was forced to rely closely on his warrior training.

Arrow Keeper had constantly emphasized the dangers of too much thinking, which distracted a man when he ought to be attending to the signals from his senses. Now, with vision practically useless, Touch the Sky freed his mind of thoughts and paid attention to the language outside of him.

He kept his ears pricked for the slightest noise.

But he heard only the hollow shrieking of the wind—no hidden horses snuffling, no bit-rings clinking, no rifle bolts snicking home in the darkness above him. Nevertheless, more sweat broke out on his back with every step he took.

He sniffed the air carefully and constantly, alert for the familiar smell of horses, the stink of unwashed human bodies.

Nothing. Just the clean, damp smell of the mountain. Still his skin grew goosebumped as if he were lying naked in a snowbank.

Shadows seemed to move in and out of the distorted periphery of the trail. But the lazy feathers of steam made it impossible to tell what was real and what wasn't. Everything was dream-distorted, so he couldn't tell how close or far things were.

Suddenly a pebble fell near his feet.

Had he kicked it loose?

Another pebble, and now fear coated his tongue in a coppery dust. For he had recalled something, a "game" Sis-ki-dee had once played with him when Touch the Sky had sighted the railroad spur through the Sans Arcs. The renegade had remained in hiding, tossing pebbles and making rattlesnake sounds to unnerve the Cheyenne, letting him know that he was a mere bug inching along the face of the mountain—a bug he could flick off at any moment.

Just as he could flick him off again now.

Nature often seems to abet the schemes of men. Now, even before Touch the Sky could fight down the blind panic caused by his helplessness, a hard wind whipped up and simultaneously pushed the clouds away from the moon while also parting the tendrils of ghostly mist.

Just enough for Touch the Sky to see that he was completely ringed in by a grinning Sis-ki-dee and his well-armed warriors!

Chapter Seven

"So! Once again the Contrary Warrior comes face to face with the noble champion of red pride! I promised you, the last time I saw you, that our trails would cross again soon enough. And see, I have kept my word!"

It was a tableau from a nightmare. Touch the Sky saw that familiar visage, mocking and ravaged by smallpox, as it seemed to float toward him out of the swirling, moonlit mists. But the Cheyenne held his face impassive, kept his tone defiant, as he answered.

"You did indeed make that promise. But you spoke those brave words even as you fled for your life."

"That was then, this is now. I also promised," Sis-ki-dee added, the mocking grin easing into a wide smile of triumph, "that I would skin your face off and lay it over mine with you still alive to see it. That time has come, Ghost Warrior. Or would you turn our bullets into sand even now, as the superstitious Cheyenne grandmothers claim you once did to Bluecoats in the Bear Paw Mountains?"

"I need not bother," Touch the Sky replied, "so long as my own bullets are real."

What followed was a move of pure desperation. Touch the Sky suddenly whirled and shot point-blank at the nearest brave. The round struck just above his navel and blew an exit hole the size of a fist in the man's back. The shot was still ringing in the damp air when the Cheyenne jumped through the space left open when the brave dropped dead.

It took less than two seconds. By the time the surprised Blackfoot renegades realized it, the tall Cheyenne had slipped from their net and back into the swirling vapors.

"Capture him!" Touch the Sky heard Sis-ki-dee bellow. His voice was tense from fear of losing this prize catch. "Good whiskey and white man's tobacco for the brave who tackles him!"

The tall youth bolted with reckless abandon into the protective but disorienting steam. His feet landed hard on sharp flints; twice he banged hard into big boulders and almost went down. His flight was reckless now as he heard the pursuing feet behind him.

Rifles cracked, bullets splatted hard or whanged

from rock to rock, zwipping close to his ears. His wild retreat took on all the features of a fever delirium: objects were obscured in vision, sounds distorted, directions nonexistent in this eerie and warm fog. He knew his men below could hear the guns discharging, perhaps even see the brief muzzle-flashes. But they were holding their fire, fearful of hitting Touch the Sky in the steam and confusion.

A bullet struck so close it sent rock dust into his eyes. Touch the Sky groped blindly, fell hard, felt himself tumbling downslope; it was like being kicked over and over in all the vital places. Then somehow he was back on his feet, bloodied and limping, groping ever downward as bullets continued to thicken the air around him.

"Brother! Do you hear me?"

Little Horse's desperate voice was somewhere just ahead.

"I hear you!" Touch the Sky managed to shout back.

"We are covered down and ready, Cheyenne! As soon as you break clear, tuck low and stay down, for the air will be humming above knee level!"

Even as Little Horse finished speaking, Touch the Sky hurtled forward from the necklace of ghostly steam. He had a momentary glimpse of his fellow warriors in their defensive positions among the scree. Then he was on the ground, and his four companions turned that steam dangerous when they opened fire.

The rifle shots found only boulders. But Little Horse made all four of his barrels roar, the scattergun peppering the pale vapor with deadly buckshot.

Loosing an agonized scream, one Blackfoot renegade dropped like a stone right beside Touch the Sky. Nothing was left of his face but a scarlet smear. Another caught buckshot in his belly and stumbled. Touch the Sky had his obsidian knife out in a heartbeat. He rolled fast toward the renegade and caught him even as he started to rise again. The Cheyenne sliced his throat open before his enemy could rise past the first knee.

The unexpected resistance broke the Blackfoot attack. But any further advance by the Cheyennes was clearly impossible. Battered, sore, but grateful to have breath in his nostrils still after that harrowing escape, Touch the Sky joined his band in a retreat down Wendigo Mountain.

"We killed at least two of them," Little Horse boasted, rallying the others. "True, Touch the Sky here forgot his name and touched the ground more than the sky—one time too many, from the look of his cuts and bruises. But his blade made a Blackfoot dog's throat bay at the moon! And here we stand, while our enemy are two less! They call us the Fighting Cheyenne, and they are right to do so."

"We stopped them," Touch the Sky agreed. "You turned your shotgun into a Bluecoat regiment. But I know this crazy killer Sis-ki-dee, and so do you, Little Horse. You fought him and his men. You know he is not one for a hoop-and-pole game, where each side makes its move in turn."

"Straight words. I learned he is called the Contrary Warrior because he prefers to strike on his own terms, in his own time."

Touch the Sky nodded. "Honor and the Warrior Way mean nothing to him. There is no soft place in him. He once bragged of braining an infant against a tree, making its mother die on the spot of shock and grief. No man who can speak of such a thing while smiling deserves to live."

The Cheyennes had returned to their meager camp in the foothills. Attack from the mountain was unlikely, since only one clear path, the narrow trace down the southern slope, led to their camp. The Cheyennes took turns on sentry duty, the rest managing only fitful sleep.

As a new dawn limned the eastern horizon, no one said it directly. But all were aware: Only two sleeps remained until the all-important deadline.

Touch the Sky knew this mission would be desperate under the best of conditions. With the present urgency, however, it took on the face of sheer madness. Each man had spoken in a grim battle council. They agreed on one important point: They would never get up that slope alive. And their deaths, no matter how glorious, would do nothing to return those Arrows.

"Yes, and Sis-ki-dee has found the right home," Little Horse agreed. "For he is the very Wendigo himself and has nothing to fear from this accursed place."

"He has Cheyennes to fear," Touch the Sky reminded them. "And count upon it, brothers, he fears us. He is too smart not to."

The new sun gave off little light, but embers still glowed in the firepit. Touch the Sky had been studying Arrow Keeper's pictograph. A sinking realization had come to him as he puzzled over the crude painting of the eagle. He studied it again, then gazed back over his shoulder toward the mountain. One eye was swollen shut from his tumble down the talus slope.

Little Horse watched his friend.

"What is it, brother? You suddenly look like a much older Indian."

"And feel like one, buck, for I think I now understand more of the meaning of Arrow Keeper's warning."

"If you understand it better, then why not smile, for it must also mean you have a plan for us?"

The rest watched him expectantly.

"A pale sort of plan," Touch the Sky reluctantly conceded.

"Nothing is as pale as nothing, buck! And nothing is all we have. Speak this plan."

"Did you notice, when we made our scout around the mountain, the many eagles nesting on the northern face?"

Little Horse and the others nodded.

"In the cliffs," Little Horse added, making it a flat reminder, not a question.

"In the cliffs. See Arrow Keeper's eagle-tail feather?" Touch the Sky stated.

"Eagles nest in cliffs," Tangle Hair said slowly, catching on but reluctant to accept it. "And eagles are symbols of warriors."

"You have seized my words before I shaped them, Tangle Hair. Words I am reluctant to speak. For I am nearly certain that Arrow Keeper is telling us there is only one way up Wendigo Mountain—by scaling those same cliffs that killed our ancients."

Less than one full sleep to the southeast, at Gray Thunder's camp, Wolf Who Hunts Smiling was up early, too. He and Medicine Flute had met in the common corral. Pretending to work their ponies, they could easily speak frank words without fear of unfriendly ears overhearing them.

"Brother," Wolf Who Hunts Smiling said. "In my haste not to get caught with the Arrows, I was a bit too quick to get rid of them."

Medicine Flute stood idle and watched his friend while he lunged his pure black pony, leading it in tight circles by a buffalo-hair rope tied to its hackamore. He ignored his own pony, a scrawny dun with flat withers. The dun's lack of muscle definition contrasted sharply with the black's. Bored by horses, the slender, sleepy-eyed youth instead played an eerie and toneless melody on his flute, made from a hollowed-out human leg bone. He pulled the instrument from his lips long enough to say, "Too quick to get rid of the Arrows? How so?"

"I was drunk at the prospect of finally possessing the means to kill White Man Runs Him. In two sleeps, that will be done. But even better if, after Touch the Sky's head is offered, the brave I chose as our only true shaman were to somehow magically return the Arrows after Sis-ki-dee refused."

"I like the sound of this," Medicine Flute said. "But tell me a thing. Do you believe this Sis-ki-dee ever planned to return them?"

Wolf Who Hunts Smiling flashed the lupine grin that had earned him his name.

"Your thoughts run with mine. I was a fool to think he would. But truly I would like to have that crazy-eyed Contrary Warrior in my battle camp, if possible. So I will talk about the matter with him. But I will also watch for a way to lay hands on those Arrows myself. The shaman whose magic returned them to our clan circles unsullied would rule over the tribe until his death."

"Yes," Medicine Flute agreed softly, "until his death."

Wolf Who Hunts Smiling saw the gleam of ambition in his companion's eyes. Good. It was ambition, and ambition alone, that could grasp the reins of leadership and drive an entire tribe. Medicine Flute was lazy, and if not an actual coward, he was certainly no warrior. But he was crafty enough to understand that an Indian blessed with big medicine never lacked for new moccasins and tender hump steaks.

As for Wolf Who Hunts Smiling, he was weary of this constant cat-and-mouse game. He and Touch the Sky had tested, tormented, and probed each other's vulnerable places while they waited for the right moment to close for the kill.

Wolf Who Hunts Smiling had powerful dreams of glory. When he was still a child playing war with willow-branch shields, he used to watch the chiefs and soldier-troop leaders ride at the head of the Sun Dance parades. Their war bonnets, heavy with coup feathers, trailed out behind them. And they held their faces stern and proud as the people pointed in awe—for were they not warriors who must maintain an aloof dignity around women and children?

Now, mere dreams of glory were no longer sufficient. There was a gnawing in his belly, a cankering need for power and respect.

"Brother," he said, gazing out toward the serried peaks of the Sans Arc range, "this Touch the Sky and his fawning admirers have cost me my coup feathers! When our women and children were seized during the hunt, his group rescued them and made mine look like squaw men.

"Recently, he has become the pet of many. They say he defeated the white buffalo hiders, using magic to make Uncle Pte stampede on them. They say that he restored our trade goods after killing a tyrant on the Cherokee reservation."

Wolf Who Hunts Smiling dropped his distant gaze to Medicine Flute's eyes.

"All along I have swallowed this bitter bile, yet see how I still smile? For now he has lost our tribe's most sacred possession."

"As you say. And with Arrow Keeper gone, few are willing to pet this dog now."

Wolf Who Hunts Smiling nodded at this. "If Sis-ki-dee has not already killed him, it will happen soon enough by his own hand."

"He would fall on his own knife?"

Again Wolf Who Hunts Smiling nodded.

"I know this tall buck well. Once he fails to get those Arrows, his noble sense of 'honor' will drive him to it."

"Depriving you," Medicine Flute said, "of that pleasure."

"True it is, I would like the pleasure of gutting him. But this way I come out with a clean blade to show the Councillors, yet *he* will be dead."

Chapter Eight

"They are leaving us alone," Touch the Sky said. "But they are like hawks who keep their prey in sight long before they swoop for the kill. They know by now that we have this camp in the foothills. They are watching it. So we will make it appear as if we were still here even after we have started our climb. With luck, we may throw them off a little."

Little Horse and the rest nodded. Leaving false camps behind had saved them before. While the afternoon sun blazed down from a seamless blue sky, they worked back out of sight of the sentry posts on the slope.

They built up fires that would burn far into the night. Limbs were stacked so that they would roll onto the fire as the smaller sticks holding them back were burned away, a crude system of time-released deception they had learned from the wily Comanche. They also left mounds near the fire to simulate the shapes of seated and sleeping bodies. The remounts were left there to graze.

As they moved closer to Wendigo Mountain, they kept back in the aspen and cedar groves so their motion wouldn't be detected by the sentries at their stations on the slope.

"I found a place up ahead to tether our ponies," Shoots the Bear said. He had ridden out earlier to scout for grazing land. "It is not far enough away to suit me. It is a short ride beyond the northern face. A small meadow bordered by a rill. Our ponies will not be safe from a scout, but they cannot be seen from the southern slope."

"It will have to do," Touch the Sky told him. "You found the best place you could."

A grim sense of purpose marked the faces of each brave. They had paid close attention to those daunting cliffs during their initial scout of the mountain. Now, as they slipped past them again on their way to the hidden meadow, Touch the Sky and the rest craned their necks to look upward.

The sheer, rugged, breathtaking beauty was wasted on these Cheyennes who would never see this place as a gift of the High Holy Ones. Bluff faces of stone stretched steeply upward, offering few shelves or ledges to provide rest for weary climbers. Back here, too, the white collar of steam ringed the mountain about halfway up. Nor could any of them deny the fear that lay in their bellies with a leaden heaviness, the strong tribal fear of this place where the Wendigo lay in wait to snare foolish Cheyennes.

"Two Twists," Touch the Sky warned the youngest brave. "Keep your pony to the trees. If a Blackfoot spots us back here and guesses our plan, we will be picked off the mountain like nits from a blanket."

"Better than dying like old women in our tipis," Two Twists shot back. "I am ready."

Little Horse grinned at this bravado. Two Twist's warlike attitude was starting to show.

Touch the Sky joined them in their grin. But he made sure Two Twists was listening when he replied, "Only fools rush to a quick death. An old woman who dies in her tipi has had a long life. A long life is nothing to scorn, so you keep your honor in the living of it."

But now they fell silent as they reached the hidden meadow and turned their ponies loose on long rawhide tethers. By the time they had rigged for battle and the long climb, their shadows had lengthened behind them. The final task was a careful inspection of the braided buffalo-hair ropes coiled around them like brassards. Weak spots were reinforced with tendon. A weak rope could mean disaster for all of them on that unholy cliff.

"We are as ready as we have time to be," Touch the Sky finally announced. "Only one thing remains."

He pulled a blunt piece of charcoal from his parfleche and went around to each brave in turn, marking his face with bold black strokes—the symbol of joy in the death of an enemy.

"We have a hard climb ahead," he told them, "and most likely a bloody fight waits for us at the top. But you all know it as well as I. The fate of those Arrows is the fate of our tribe. This time there can be no turning back. So from here on out, let our thoughts be bloody and nothing else."

By the time Sister Sun had burned down to a dull orange ball on the western horizon, the five Powder River Cheyennes were up against it in the truest sense of the words.

They had sneaked up to the base of Wendigo Mountain's northern face, quickly hiding in the scree. Then began the arduous climb up those sheer cliffs.

The work was dangerous and exhausting, and at the beginning Touch the Sky—in spite of his bold words earlier—almost called off this crazy plan. But each time he thought of that, Little Horse's words returned to him, a hint from Arrow Keeper's medicine dream: *There will be trouble ahead for Touch the Sky, trouble behind for Honey Eater*. And the young warrior had learned one thing well by now: Trouble never went away on its own if you ran from it. You either had to take it by the horns or suffer a hard goring.

Progress was slow, every finger-length eked out

at the cost of much sweat and toil. Touch the Sky went up first, clawing for handholds, groping constantly for toeholds on the smooth limestone expanse. Each time he reached a spur or occasional stunted tree or bush, he carefully tested its strength. Then he secured a rope to it. Little Horse followed next, then Two Twists, Tangle Hair, and Shoots the Bear.

Salty, stinging sweat beaded up on his scalp and then rolled into his eyes. The fierce winds fanned the sweat, causing him to shake.

A few inches, another foot, and now the cliff face was so smooth it seemed as if further advance was impossible. But Touch the Sky refused to give up. Fingers and toes seeming to make their own holds, he somehow inched his way up that smooth stretch.

But Little Horse—not quite so agile of limb— was stuck, along with the others behind him.

Touch the Sky knew he had to get a rope snubbed to something or this mission was smoke behind them. A moment later, he realized things were even more desperate than that.

"Brother!" Little Horse called up to him, his voice sounding tiny in the immensity of the constant wind. "I am losing my hold!"

Touch the Sky glanced down and felt his blood go cold. Little Horse was literally hanging on by his last leg. From here, he was hunched up like a bug about to tumble.

"Can you move back down?" Touch the Sky called out.

"No! I fear I would slip and knock the others down, too!"

"You are a fighting Cheyenne, buck! Hold but a bit longer, brother, and I'll have a rope down to you."

Touch the Sky's mouth formed a grim, determined slit. Muscles straining like taut cables, he scrabbled for some kind of hold. Above, perhaps ten handbreadths away, he spotted a small rock spur. If only he could reach it in time! But his promise to Little Horse was proving easier to shout than to carry out.

"Brother!"

This time Little Horse's voice was strained with fear and effort. Touch the Sky risked another glance down. His friend desperately hugged the cliff face, but the increasing gusts of wind threatened at every moment to tear him loose and hurtle him to the basalt turrets far below.

"Brother!" he cried out again. "I fear this is it, my time to cross over is at hand. I can hold no longer. I will have to leap now to avoid hitting the others."

"Hold!" Touch the Sky shouted back. "I will have a rope down in a little."

Desperation welled up inside him. How many times had his loyal, sturdy little friend pulled him from the jaws of death? Even now, about to crash to a hard death, all Little Horse could worry about was protecting his brothers.

Touch the Sky grasped, clawed, somehow found holds where none existed. His fingernails had torn loose long ago. Spidery lines of blood spread from his fingertips all the way down his arms. But now the rock spur was just above him.

Then his bones turned to stone when he heard Little Horse chanting the death song!

Touch the Sky unlooped his rope, flung it up toward the spur, missed.

He wasn't even aware that he cursed in English. He threw the rope up again, snared the spur this time. Fingers working with desperate competence, he knotted the rope.

"Little Horse!" he shouted, dropping the rope toward his friend just before Little Horse lost his battle with the cliff. He flung himself back away from it, falling so he wouldn't strike the others on his way down.

The rope slapped Little Horse in mid-air just before he began to plummet. He instinctively grabbed at it, missed, grabbed again; a moment later it snapped taut, held, and Little Horse dangled safe though somewhat shaken from the impact when he swung back into the face of the cliff.

It was a slow, agonizing process getting him and the rest of them up. Each man in turn climbed to the level of the rock spur, then threw the rope down to the next man. When Shoots the Bear was safely up, Touch the Sky began covering the next expanse of cliff.

By now his arms trembled with weariness. The Cheyennes inched closer toward the belt of steam. Once again the nimble young brave covered a smooth expanse of cliff while his companions hung on for dear life and waited for the rope.

Touch the Sky reached a tiny ledge the width of perhaps three fingers. He hauled himself up, hugged the stone face, again snubbed his rope around a rock spur. He had partially completed the knot when disaster struck.

Touch the Sky had already noticed the slight cleft in the otherwise solid rock wall. But he didn't realize it was a falcon's nest until a startled bird flew out from the cleft and full into Touch the Sky's face—knocking him from his fragile foothold on the tiny ledge.

His four companions watched in wide-eyed shock as their battle leader began the long fall to his death.

"Easy now," Sis-ki-dee told Takes His Share. "With luck, we'll beard the lion in his own den."

Sis-ki-dee imitated the fluting warble of a wood thrush, and the battle group behind him stopped in their tracks. The sky was dark but star-shot, casting a soft glow like foxfire over the trees and scattered boulders dotting the Sans Arc foothills. Below them, perhaps a double stone's throw distant, was the Cheyenne camp.

"It has a bad feel to it," Takes His Share said. "I know these white-livered Cheyennes are superstitious about leaving their fires after darkness. But would *all* of them be sleeping?"

Sis-ki-dee's sinister grin showed well that he was ahead of Takes His Share on this point.

"And have you noticed there is no sentry?" he said. "When did Cheyennes ever neglect to post a night watch?"

They advanced quickly toward the fire.

"Only two horses," Takes His Share said.

"We'll throat-slash them," Sis-ki-dee said. "Look, they're only pack nags. Our Cheyennes have played the fox, stout bucks!"

Moments later, a bloodless takeover of the camp proved the Contrary Warrior's words.

"Kill the horses," he ordered his men. "Quickly! Then prepare to ride."

"Ride where, Contrary Warrior?"

Sis-ki-dee stared back toward the looming peak of Wendigo Mountain. Even as he stared, thin filaments of lightning flashed near the granite summit. They rivaled the insane sheen of his eyes.

"Only think, warrior. Why was this camp made?"

"To divert us, clearly."

"Clearly, indeed. But divert us from what?"

Takes His Share shed much brain sweat, but only ended up shaking his head.

"It puzzles me, I confess. They cannot be ascending the slope. Half our force is watching it."

"As you say. Half are on the slope, the other half wasting time at this camp. As for our little Cheyenne foxes, they are on the far side of that mountain, defying their own Wendigo in order to surprise our camp. Let us make a fast ride to

94

those cliffs, buck, and see what surprises we may devise to outfox the foxes!"

As Touch the Sky hurtled earthward, he clung to the rope that had been only partially knotted before he fell.

There was a hard, fast snap as the rope tightened, and then a bright orange starburst inside his skull when his head slammed hard into the wall of stone. The blow didn't knock him unconscious nor cost him his grip, but Touch the Sky dangled helpless, on the feather edge of death, as his mind played cat-and-mouse with awareness.

Brother! Can you hear me? Touch the Sky!

He was on some kind of important quest, he knew that. But time and place and purpose got all mixed up in memory, and now he was again in the midst of his great vision quest to the Black Hills—the journey Arrow Keeper had sent him on to experience the same medicine dream the old shaman had once experienced.

Touch the Sky! Wake to the living world, brother!

But now the images and sounds came tumbling back, reminding him of his inescapable destiny.

The voice of Old Knobby, the hostler at the feed stable in Bighorn Falls: *The Injun figgers he belongs to the land. The white man figgers the land belongs to him. They ain't meant to live together.*

He heard John Hanchon, his adopted white father: *I've worked until I'm mule-tired, but I still go to bed scared every night.*

The words gave way to mind pictures from his vision at Medicine Lake. He saw horses rearing, their eyes huge with fright, while red warriors sang their battle cry. Rivers of blood flowed everywhere, cannons roared, steel clashed against steel. From across the vast plains red warriors streamed, flowing like the blood they must soon shed. One brave led them, his war bonnet streaming coup feathers.

Glimpses of the ice-shrouded lands to the north. He saw the faces of his enemies, Hiram Steele and Seth Carlson. He saw a long, ragged column of starving Cheyenne, again being led by the mysterious brave whose face he could not see.

This time the voice belonged to Honey Eater's dead father, Chief Yellow Bear, speaking from the Land of Ghosts:

We who have crossed over know everything that will pass. I have seen you bounce your son on your knee, just as I have seen you shed blood for that son and his mother.

A thundering crash that wasn't in memory. Abruptly Touch the Sky felt the burning in his palms as the rope slipped through them. He came fully awake just in time to grip hard and stop his fall.

"Brother!" Little Horse bellowed yet again above the angry shriek of the wind. "Can you hear me?"

"I hear you, buck!"

Another crack of thunder, ghostly white flashes

of lightning. The wind had taken on a raw knife-edge of cold now that Sister Sun was asleep.

Slowly, laboriously, every muscle crying out at the effort, Touch the Sky climbed back up to the rock spur. Heels biting into the small ledge, he finished the knot and tested it. Then he dropped the rope down to a relieved Little Horse.

Again, one by one, the braves made their way up to the tiny ledge.

"Only one last stretch!" Touch the Sky rallied them above the weather roar. By now his voice was hoarse from the effort. "Through the steam, and then we have a slope for footing the rest of the way."

His loose black locks swirled like living snakes in the tempest. They all watched as Shoots the Bear, the last and heaviest brave, climbed the rope to join them.

Touch the Sky and Little Horse both reached down to hoist him. His fingers met Touch the Sky's and started to close, and then a heartbeat later the rock spur snapped.

It was just a fast noise like a strong bone breaking. Touch the Sky closed his hand on thin air as Shoots the Bear's hideous death shriek melded with the wind.

Chapter Nine

While the moon inched toward its zenith, Sis-ki-dee and his renegade band rode hard toward the northern face of Wendigo Mountain.

At first they noticed nothing unusual. No signs of enemy ponies or any camp. Nor, in the moonless night, could they see very far up those sheer cliffs.

"Perhaps my thoughts flew too quickly to the cliffs," Sis-ki-dee confided to Takes His Share. "But if that tall Cheyenne licker of white men's crotches is not coming up this way, then how? Will he sprout wings?"

"Certainly not by the southern slope," Takes His Share said with conviction. "Not one shot has been fired from that direction."

Sis-ki-dee's men had lit torches to scour the

rocks. Sis-ki-dee sat his big claybank, watching them and brooding. Eerie, flickering light reflected off the fancy silver trim of his stolen saddle. It also emphasized the numerous facial craters of his smallpox scars, the mad gleam to his eyes.

"Then how?" Sis-ki-dee repeated. "Where is he? For count upon it, that one will not hide in his tipi while his tribe's Sacred Arrows are in enemy hands."

Suddenly a shout went up from Sioux Killer, a brave searching in the heaps of scree in front of them.

"Contrary Warrior! Here is a thing you will want to see. Come quickly!"

The Blackfoot swung down and hobbled his horse's foreleg to rear. Then he picked his way over the scattered piles of rock, aiming for the flickering illumination of Sioux Killer's torch.

Abruptly, Sis-ki-dee pulled up short.

He stared at the place where Sioux Killer pointed. Then his jaw slacked open in surprise. But only moments later, a huge smile divided his face.

The torch clearly illuminated a short and narrow basalt turret which ended in a sharp point. And there, skewered through the vitals about sixteen handbreadths above the ground, was a Cheyenne warrior wearing a hideous death grimace.

"I was right," he said triumphantly. "They have decided to climb up from this side."

"But it is a fool's plan," Takes His Share said.

"Not so much foolish as desperate, brave. But that hardly matters. For as this one proves eloquently enough, those cliffs cannot be scaled."

"Not by most Indians, perhaps. But that Cheyenne does things other red men cannot."

Sis-ki-dee readily acknowledged the truth of this with a nod.

"He does, doesn't he? But even if he could make the climb, no one is in our camp. Turn it over all he will, he'll never find those Arrows."

Sis-ki-dee continued to stare at the grotesque dead man. The pain etched into his face defied description. Looking at it inspired Sis-ki-dee to mischief.

His strong white teeth flashed in the flickering light when the idea occurred to him. For Sis-ki-dee, defeating his enemies was not nearly enough retribution. Life was meant to be an entertainment; mere victory was boring. If at all possible, he preferred to terrorize his quarry before killing it. He turned to Takes His Share.

"Pick several strong braves and remove that body. Do not harm it. I want it left intact. Tie it to a horse."

"Why, Contrary Warrior?"

Again Sis-ki-dee flashed his crazy-by-thunder grin. He pointed to the dead Cheyenne.

"Do you think this one died hard? We will make his tall leader's life a hurting place. Quickly now! In case he does somehow survive the climb, we must have a surprise ready to welcome the Noble Red Man and his braves."

The night was well advanced, and to the north of the Powder River camp lightning crowned the Sans Arc mountain range. Black Elk, his cousin Wolf Who Hunts Smiling, and Medicine Flute sat around a small fire behind Black Elk's tipi.

Black Elk was plaiting a new bridle out of rawhide and horsehair. Medicine Flute had taken a rare break from the incessant piping on his leg-bone flute. Now he sat peeling a twig with his teeth, his sleepy, heavy-lidded gaze directed into the leaping flames while Wolf Who Hunts Smiling spoke.

"Cousin, fear has our tribe by the throat. Two sleeps from now Woman Face's head is due in payment for the Medicine Arrows. Yet, where is he? Many are starting to wonder a thing. What happens if this dog decides to tuck his tail and flee?"

Black Elk nodded.

"He is no coward. But neither is he loyal to the Cheyenne way. For all we know, he is rabbiting to safety even now. Meantime, we cannot attack for fear of endangering the Arrows."

"Never, not since the time when he was accused of helping the white miners steal our lands, has there been so much talk against him. I have been speaking with the people, telling them about Medicine Flute. How his medicine is strong along with his loyalty to the tribe."

Wolf Who Hunts Smiling paused, recalling some past slight that made him scowl.

"Now the people are saying, no more of this business with tolerating a shaman who was raised by hair faces. Arrow Keeper is gone, perhaps dead by now. True, I will not have the pleasure of using Touch the Sky's guts for tipi ropes. But we have finally had done with White Man Runs Him."

"Too early for a victory dance, buck. You have declared him dead more than once."

When he finished speaking, Black Elk's eyes cut toward his tipi. All was dark within. But was Honey Eater really asleep, or was she listening for news to send to her tall buck?

Let her listen, he decided angrily. Her blunt coldness with him, her brazen disrespect ever since Touch the Sky rode out, had worked him up to a murderous rage. How dare a mere woman lord it over a war leader! No woman turned Black Elk into a squaw man and lived to boast about it.

Again, as the anger bubbled up inside him, the thought cankered at him. Had Honey Eater let the tall dog lift her dress?

Wolf Who Hunts Smiling cast a furtive, sidelong glance at his cousin. He saw Black Elk scowling as he stared at the tipi.

"Cousin," Wolf Who Hunts Smiling said, "we spoke earlier on a certain matter. I have held council with several bucks. All reliable, all respected. They have agreed to come forward, if you give the sign. They will swear on the

Medicine Hat that they saw Touch the Sky hold"—
here he glanced at Medicine Flute and decided to
avoid Honey Eater's name—"a certain woman in
his blanket for love talk."

Black Elk said nothing to this, though he
took the meaning clearly enough. Something
else was troubling him. Lately he had expended
much brain sweat wondering how this Blackfoot
renegade named Sis-ki-dee had obtained those
Arrows. Touch the Sky would always carry the
white stink on him, truly. But in his secret heart of
hearts, Black Elk did not believe he was a traitor.
He had not voluntarily given those Arrows away.

How, then, did Sis-ki-dee get them?

He watched his sly, ambitious cousin in the
firelight. Would he place his dreams of glory
before the well-being of the entire tribe?

Wolf Who Hunts Smiling had already come
dangerously close to unpardonable treachery in
an earlier scheme with Medicine Flute. The two
had cleverly challenged Touch the Sky's right to
the title of shaman, engaging in deceptions and
lies unknown to the Council of Forty. Black Elk
had reluctantly gone along with it, hoping to
expose Touch the Sky as a pretend shaman. But
the resourceful brave used strong magic to defeat
the Comanche trick rider Big Tree, emerging with
even more supporters.

Truly Black Elk wanted this Touch the Sky,
this dog who might have rutted with his wife,
dead. Just as his jealous visions of Honey Eater
lying with Touch the Sky had finally driven him

to want her dead, too. But not at the terrible expense of the entire tribe's well-being. Black Elk would not go that far.

Even now the wily Wolf Who Hunts Smiling discerned some of these thoughts in his cousin's troubled frown. It was burning ambition versus stupid loyalty, and Wolf Who Hunts Smiling was confident that his ambition would win out. By goading Black Elk into killing Honey Eater, Wolf Who Hunts Smiling also strengthened his own position. For then he would have power over Black Elk. He would know a damaging secret about a truly dangerous man. If Black Elk could not be won over, then he must at least be knocked from his position of authority.

"Count upon it, cousin," Wolf Who Hunt Smiling said. "True it is, the loss of our Arrows is a great tragedy. We have yet to learn the terrible consequences of this loss. But every strong wind blows something good before it, too. This tragedy also marks the end for White Man Runs Him."

Shoots the Bear's unexpected death stunned the remaining Cheyennes into disbelieving silence.

For many heartbeats they clung where they were, four tiny specks of humanity pinned to the vast face of the treacherous and indifferent cliff. Thunder muttered, lightning flickered, the wind carried a cold promise of rain. Truly it was a bad death, the worst conceivable to a Cheyenne. Not only did their comrade die in a place fraught with evil medicine, but he died unclean, unable to sing his death song.

It was more than a bad death. It was also a bad omen, a serious warning to the rest of them.

But fear, Touch the Sky reminded himself, was no defense. Only action would save the rest of them—and, more important, the Arrows. He glanced up and noted the location of the Always Star to the north. The night was advancing, and so must they. Now he spoke, careful to avoid the dead brave's name.

"Brothers! The one who was our comrade died bad. But now *we* are up against it. More death will not save the one who has left us. Nor will it save the Sacred Arrows."

Or Honey Eater, a sere, gravelly voice remarkably like Arrow Keeper's whispered out of the howling wind.

"Now comes the last climb. Be strong, and take heart. From here the going is easier. There are more holds and places to rest. We will not even need the ropes."

"We are with you, Bear Caller!" Little Horse shouted above the shriek of savage winds.

He used the name terrified Pawnees gave Touch the Sky after a grizzly bear routed them and saved his life.

"Our brother died giving his all to the tribe," Little Horse added. "What better way can a Cheyenne die? We are pledged to the same sacrifice, if Maiyun wills it. As for me, I have no dream of a long life. Lead on, buck, for I am keen to grease Blackfoot bones with my war paint!"

Little Horse's brave words rallied his comrades. And Touch the Sky had spoken straight-arrow: from here the going was easier. Even the climb through the steamy mist was uneventful, even pleasant, as the tendrils of warm steam thawed their cold skin.

But Touch the Sky could not rid himself of the coppery taste of fear. For this was Wendigo Mountain, where any kind of bad medicine might happen. And in Sis-ki-dee, they were not just up against an enemy—this was a murdering, marauding, implacable beast who truly thrived on evil.

He had little luxury for thought, however, because now he was approaching the summit of the cliff. All seemed quiet enough up above. But what if Sis-ki-dee had discovered their bold plan? What if, even now, his battle-hardened renegades lay in wait to slaughter them?

He held up until his comrades flanked him just beneath the top of the sheer face. A line of rimrock was all that kept them from the rest of the talus-strewn northern face. One more open space to cross, and they would be on the opposite slope and above the Blackfoot camp.

Touch the Sky placed an arm over his comrades' shoulders, huddling them close. He spoke just loud enough to top the wind noise.

"Spread out wide, brothers. We will go over together on my signal. Tangle Hair, hand me that scalp on your sash."

Tangle Hair unknotted a rawhide whang and handed the Pawnee scalp to his battle leader. The others watched, quickly catching on, as Touch the Sky tied the scalp to the muzzle of his Sharps. Then, cautiously, he raised it above the rimrock. Only the dark hair showed. But no shots were lured.

"They are there or they are not," Touch the Sky said. "If they are there, make it one bullet for one enemy!"

He slung his rifle across his shoulders and crawled over the rimrock. The rest, spread out on either side, topped the cliff with him.

Touch the Sky believed he was prepared for anything. But nothing between this living world and the Land of Ghosts could have prepared any of these deeply spiritual Indians for the blood-curdling sight that greeted them. For just as they reached the top, a brilliant flash of lightning turned the night into clear daylight.

Young Two Twists cried out and fell to the ground, literally struck down by fear. The rest froze where they stood.

There, his accusing eyes wide open and staring at them, a gaping and bloody hole where his stomach once had been, stood Shoots the Bear!

Chapter Ten

Absolute silence from the Cheyennes for the space of ten heartbeats. Their black locks flew about like wild sisal whips in the unrelenting wind. The bold black charcoal streaks on their faces could not offset the fear starched into their features.

Then, as realization set in, Touch the Sky felt his fear give way to hot rage.

"Stand up, Cheyenne," he told Two Twists sternly. "Be a man, for this has nothing to do with matters spiritual. Look there, and there."

Lightning flashes were almost constant now. He pointed to the rocks heaped around the legs, and to a cleverly disguised rope around the upper body, running to a hidden stake nearby. Both had been used to prop up and pose the body.

"The wily Red Peril and his murdering follow-ers found our comrade and hauled him up here."

Touch the Sky's words made the rest overcome their fear enough to glance nervously about them. The Cheyennes had finally ascended the cliffs. But between them and the final summit of Wendigo Mountain stretched a final, rock-strewn slope. The rocks were easily big enough to hide ambushers.

"Sis-ki-dee has stooped to the basest form of sacrilege in defiling our dead this way," Touch the Sky said. "But we have more urgent mat-ters to hand if our quest is for the Arrows. If they bothered to haul our dead comrade up here, clearly they knew we were on our way up.

"Cover down brothers, and quickly, for right now Sis-ki-dee must be hiding nearby and enjoy-ing his laugh at us. When his amusement wears off, comes the fight!"

Even as he finished speaking, the hideous "shout that kills" erupted, the frightening battle cry Sis-ki-dee had taught to his men. It was a shrill, deep-chested scream designed to unnerve opponents. In one movement the Blackfoot ren-egades rose from hiding and rushed them.

There was neither time nor space for falling back. Touch the Sky and his companions leaped behind boulders even as the first volley of fire turned the air deadly all around them.

Fortunately their weapons had been loaded and ready to hand. And Cheyennes, like their Sioux cousins, were notorious bullet hoarders trained to make each shot count. Touch the Sky fired a quick snapshot from his Sharps, dropping an attacker. There were sharper cracks as Tangle Hair and Two Twists fired their sturdy British trade rifles, also scoring hits.

But at this range it was once again Little Horse's revolving-barrel scattergun that truly surprised their enemy and saved them. As good as his reckless boasts, courageously tempting death, Little Horse stood in the open and jeered at his enemy.

His barrels were adjusted for the widest shot pattern. As fast as he could revolve them, he unleashed all four loads at the attackers. Blackfoot warriors dropped as if a Bluecoat canister shell had landed in their midst.

This excellent marksmanship by all four Cheyennes bought just enough time for the beleaguered braves to finish taking hasty shelter so they could reload. Knowing his bow would be more deadly at this distance and afford him more shots than his rifle, Touch the Sky notched a fire-hardened arrow on his string. His left hand gripped several more at the ready, the shafts formed from dead pine for lightness and strength.

But for the moment targets were scarce. Their enemy, stung by the quick and effective Cheyenne response, had quickly learned respect. Now they were carefully hidden, not counting their dead comrades who now littered the slope.

Next came Sis-ki-dee's insane, mocking laughter. When he spoke, it was in the mixture of Cheyenne and Sioux understood by many Plains tribes.

"Noble Red Man! If you are truly so 'noble' as you pretend, why risk your comrades like this? It is *you* Sis-ki-dee wants. Surrender, and the rest may go free. They may even take the Arrows with them."

Touch the Sky's men had no intention of letting their friend negotiate his own death. It was Tangle Hair who quickly answered, speaking for all of them.

"We came up as one. We will either leave as one or die as one. But if we die, we will fall on Blackfoot bones!"

Again came Sis-ki-dee's mocking bray.

"More noble savages! The example of your tall leader no doubt inspires you!"

"No doubt at all," Tangle Hair shot back. "He inspires me, indeed!"

Sis-ki-dee flung out an arm toward the dead Shoots the Bear.

"Is it even so? Then look on your noble and dead brother there, another who was inspired by the tall Ghost Warrior. Think carefully on my offer. For your only other choice will be to die as one! And I will personally make water on those Arrows before I destroy them."

"Then come on, Death!" Little Horse bellowed. "We are the Fighting Cheyenne! Our faces are marked black in honor of the Black Warrior's arrival!"

To taunt them, Little Horse ducked up out

of hiding for a moment and jeered at them. A second, intense volley of fire was the Blackfoot response.

Rock dust flew into Touch the Sky's eyes, bullets ricocheted around him with an ear-stinging whine. A raggedly cropped head appeared above a rock as a renegade drew a bead. Touch the Sky risked exposure long enough to loose another arrow. The fire-hardened point pierced the Blackfoot's right eye with such force it pushed gray brain-suds out the back of his skull.

"Good shot, brother!" Little Horse called over to him. "You just lightened the weight of his thoughts!"

Continuous lightning turned the battlefield into day. Sis-ki-dee's well-armed men maintained a withering field of lead. The Cheyennes could do little now but hunker down.

Desperate, but forcing himself to stay calm for the sake of his brothers, Touch the Sky signalled to Little Horse. Despite the danger, they could not stay pinned here. Retreat back down the cliff was out of the question. They must move forward and get some operating room. Otherwise, they would stay right where they were until their bullets and arrows gave out—at which time they would either join Shoots the Bear in this high-altitude grave, or die like their ancestors who had leaped off that cliff.

Touch the Sky said a brief prayer to Maiyun. Then, leading his braves in one of the most desperate and dangerous maneuvers of their young lives, he screamed the Cheyenne battle cry and broke from cover into the middle of a firestorm.

"Hi-ya! Hiii-*ya!*"

One by one, each covering the other, they advanced from rock to rock, leap-frogging through the deadly hail of bullets. Soon their faces were powder-blackened by the fierce rate of their own return fire. Repeated slaps of their rifle stocks had raised bruises on their cheekbones. Every inch of the shale-littered slope was gained at the expense of reckless valor.

Now and then Touch the Sky glimpsed Sis-ki-dee, easy to spot when lightning gleamed on his brassards or the huge brass rings in his ears. But every bullet or arrow sent toward him seemed to swerve wide as if loath to lodge in such a man-monster.

At first, despite being vastly outnumbered, the Cheyenne charge actually began to force the Blackfoot attackers into a slow retreat toward the summit. Then things began to come quickly apart like a wet rope unraveling.

Touch the Sky made occasional visual checks to make sure each of his comrades was all right. Now, just as his eyes flicked to his friend Little Horse, the plucky brave dropped his scattergun and clutched at his left shoulder. Blood spread from a new bullet hole.

Only an eyeblink later, Tangle Hair cried out as a round caught his momentarily exposed right thigh.

In the space of a breath, their firepower was cut

in half. Even though young Two Twists plugged gamely away, further advance was impossible. Only two of them were capable of moving now, and the fire from above was too deadly.

Touch the Sky saw that his companions were hastily binding their own wounds to stem the loss of blood with the strips of cloth they carried in their pouched breechclouts. Soon Tangle Hair again resumed fire, but at a slower rate than before. Little Horse, however, was unable to hold his weapons.

Two Blackfoot warriors, emboldened by this spectacle and eager to close for the kill, led a charge from the rocks. Touch the Sky shot one in the gut and left him writhing in agony; Two Twists only managed to wound the other. But it was enough to quell the assault.

For a moment there was a lull in the fierce fighting. The acrid stench of cordite hung thick in the night air. Another lightning flash, and Touch the Sky locked gazes with Sis-ki-dee.

The insane brave watched him, a triumphant sheen in his eyes. He said something to his men. Another volley of fire erupted. But this time no living man was the target. At least a dozen bullets thwapped into the body of Shoots the Bear. Held up by his props, the corpse twitched and leaped and seemed to perform a macabre dance.

"Look, contrary warriors!" Sis-ki-dee called out. "See how the Cheyenne dances to entertain us! A pity that he died without singing his death song. But little matter, for his entire tribe is soon doomed! One of them was careless, and now they have somehow misplaced their Sacred Arrows!"

Despite the desperate hopelessness of their situation, Touch the Sky felt his stomach roiling in anger. Desecration of the dead was the worst insult one tribe could heap on another. Another shot, and Shoots the Bear's head exploded like a clay pot.

Sis-ki-dee laughed long and hard.

"Settle in, Noble Cheyennes!" he called out. "We have plenty of time, ammunition, and food. Surrender the tall Ghost Warrior, and the Arrows are yours. Otherwise, first you die, then your tribe when I destroy the Arrows!"

Time dragged on. The rain held off as the sky gradually lightened toward dawn.

"Little Horse," Touch the Sky called over quietly. "How is your wound?"

The game little fighter was slow to answer. His weak tone belied the bravado of his words.

"What wound is that, brother? Do you mean this flea bite on my shoulder?"

"Tangle Hair?"

"A mere flesh wound, buck."

But his tone, too, was weak with loss of blood.

"You are both better fighters than liars," he told them.

For a moment, Touch the Sky felt the exhaustion of the long, hard climb followed by the adrenaline tension of combat. Black dots marched across his vision, and he wanted desperately to close his eyes. But, even a few moments sleep might mean sure death for all of them.

Frustrated, trying to master the weary riot of his thoughts, the tall brave carefully studied the area before him. It was littered not only with rocks and dead Blackfoot warriors but with stunted bushes twisted into grotesque shapes by the constant winds. Seeing those bushes gave him a desperate idea—foolishly desperate, a plan so risky it had almost no chance of working.

But what else was there for it? Arrow Keeper was not here to save him with magic. The situation had been dramatically altered when Little Horse and Tangle Hair were wounded. Two Twists could still move quickly, but the other two would need plenty of time to escape to safety.

Touch the Sky's warrior training and experience told him there was only one chance. He must sneak through the enemy position and somehow create an effective diversion in back of their camp, one that would flush them out long enough for his wounded comrades to gain safety.

Risking exposure several times in the almost constant glimmers of lightning, Touch the Sky used his knife to cut several of the short bushes loose. He planned to copy a trick from the Apaches to the south, masters of stealth and invisible movement.

He stripped to his clout. Slicing fringes from his buckskin leggings, he secured bushes to the back of his neck, over his buttocks, and to the back of each leg.

"Hold fast, brothers," he said quietly to the rest. "If you see your opportunity to move, seize it. Two Twists! I must leave my weapons behind. If you can, bring them when you escape."

"But where are you going?"

Ignoring their barrage of protests and curious questions, Touch the Sky inched slowly away from his position, armed only with his knife.

He hugged the ground close and moved torturously forward, trying to time his movements between lightning flashes and loud gusts of wind. Fear left his mouth feeling stuffed with cotton. But he continued to crawl forward.

It was a long, dangerous ordeal. At every moment he expected a bullet to send him across the Great Divide. He kept himself flat to the ground and made no unnecessary movements. At one point, his body drenched in nervous sweat, a swarm of gnats covered his face and almost choked him. But his lips formed their grim, determined slit and he refused to swat them.

He was unable to gauge his progress except by sound. Gradually, Blackfoot voices grew louder and louder, then softer and softer until he could hear them no longer. Then he knew that he had managed to slip past his enemy.

Touch the Sky rose cautiously just past the summit, his cramped muscles protesting.

He could see the Blackfoot stronghold below on the southern face of Wendigo Mountain.

Touch the Sky took heart when he saw that the camp was deserted. No doubt Sis-ki-dee had left another force further down this slope in case the Powder River Cheyennes tried to send a second force up.

He slipped quickly into the camp. As tempting as it was to search for the Arrows now, he resisted the urge. Every moment he delayed might mean death for his comrades—a risk he might take if the Cheyenne truly believed that Sis-ki-dee was foolish enough to hide the Medicine Arrows where they would be quickly found. But Touch the Sky knew better.

No, first things first. For now he needed a diversion. And he found one soon.

The Blackfoot stronghold was a tight cluster of tipis and curved wickiups with a common corral off to one side. A huge fire in the middle of camp had burned down to bright embers. Well back from the fire, in an area reserved for supplies, sat a case of 200 rifle cartridges.

Touch the Sky grabbed a glowing stick from the fire and raced among the tipis, setting fire where he landed. Then, moving swiftly, he upended the case of cartridges into the fire.

This move was dangerous, for he would have only a few seconds before those bullets started sending lead all around the area. He raced to a line of cedar trees below camp. Anyone spotting him at that moment might have quailed in fear: Touch the Sky still wore the bushes, which flapped like clumsy wings as he ran. And his charcoal-smeared face looked ferocious in the gathering light.

Just as he reached the shelter of the cedar brake, pandemonium broke out in the camp.

The air bristled with the sound of a fierce battle. Rounds sang through the trees, shattered branches, shredded through the tipis and wicki-ups. Several horses in the nearby common corral dropped, blood spuming from their wounds. Now it was finally light enough to see the black billows of smoke rise into the sky from the burning camp.

Despite his utter exhaustion, despite everything he still faced, Touch the Sky felt his lips easing into a grin. He had created a wonderful semblance of a massed attack. And sure enough, he could see Sis-ki-dee racing down the slope, North and Savage rifle at a high port, his men trailing out behind him.

"I have done my best, brothers," Touch the Sky said aloud, urging his comrades on. "Now do it!"

Chapter Eleven

Honey Eater was mercifully unaware of the fierce battle that Touch the Sky and his comrades had fought during the night. Nonetheless, she had enough serious worries tangling her brain to ensure that she spent a sleepless night.

At the first pale glimmer of dawn, which was visible through the smokehole at the top of the tipi, an old grandmother sang the song to the rising sun. Honey Eater rolled out of her robes, naked save for her delicate bone choker. She slipped on a buckskin dress and stepped into her moccasins.

She didn't need to worry about waking Black Elk. Like most Indian braves, he was a late and heavy sleeper when he was in a peace camp. She could see him now, on the other side of the tipi's tall center pole. Pale light filtered through the smokehole and lay across his face. Even in his sleep, she noticed with a tiny shiver, he scowled as if riding into battle.

She stood there a moment and remembered a time when she had felt differently toward Black Elk. No, he had never made her smile inside as Touch the Sky did. He was covered with hard bark, cold and remote and obsessed with warfare and his warrior pride. This unreasoning pride had led to savage jealousy now turned murderous. But there had been a time when Black Elk had at least been fair, or had tried to be, toward Touch the Sky, just as there had once been a time when Black Elk would never have cut off her braid to shame her, or beat her with the bullwhip tucked into his sash.

But those days were long gone, a thing of smoke blown behind them. And now she and Black Elk no longer lived as man and wife. Though it was important to Black Elk's manly pride that they keep up outward appearances, he had lately taken to sleeping in his own robes on the opposite side of the tipi.

One of Honey Eater's cousins had whispered a thing in her ear, a story that Black Elk now rode out 'hunting' so often because he was topping a young widow from Straight Pine's Arapaho camp. If true, this was a great relief to Honey Eater. Black Elk considered a true man to be a volcano—he must regularly relieve the pressure between his legs or he would explode. And she could no longer abide his touch.

But truly, it also worried her. For lately, Black Elk had harbored a cold and menacing indifference toward her that somehow seemed more dangerous than his rages.

Something brutal was in the wind. She was sure of it. All these meetings lately out by the meat racks with Wolf Who Hunts Smiling and the rest of Black Elk's Bull Whip brothers—they could only mean trouble, and plenty of it. Trouble for Touch the Sky, certainly. But lately she sensed that Black Elk's wrath had finally begun to include her in his cold-blooded schemes of murder.

The slender girl slipped past the entrance flap, still braiding her hair, her face lost in troubled thought. Just then, glancing down toward the mist-covered river, she spotted a doe and fawn. The doe fondly nuzzled her offspring, and for a moment Honey Eater smiled.

Her offspring . . . it was common knowledge what Black Elk had said to some in his lodge. Things about how a squaw could harden her heart toward a man, thus denying his seed from fertilizing inside her. Many of the Bull Whips believed this and goaded him on. His bitterness at her inability—some called it a refusal—to give him a son was deep. It grew deeper as time passed and more and more jokes were made about Black Elk's manhood.

But abruptly she was startled out of her musing by the angry scolding of jays. Now, as she knelt to stir the embers under the cooking tripod, more immediate troubles came crowding back.

One sleep.

One sleep, and Touch the Sky's life was forfeit if he could not return those Sacred Arrows! Of course Honey Eater was frightened, like all the others in camp, by this threat to the Arrows. The fate of those Arrows shaped the destiny of the tribe.

But Touch the Sky did not, *would* not, cause their loss. She was sure of that. As sure as she was the daughter of one of the greatest chiefs in Cheyenne history. The treacherous Wolf Who Hunts Smiling was behind this terrible trouble. He and perhaps that sly, lazy 'shaman' with the grisly bone flute.

Honey Eater stoked up the flames, then went out back to the meat racks and selected an elk steak for Black Elk's breakfast. By the time she returned, a group of women were gathering in the middle of camp. It was the custom to go out in the cool of early morning. They would scoop ants from the anthills near the river, wash them, then crush them to a paste that would be made into a tasty soup.

This reminded her that life went on because it had to. The hunters rode out, the women gathered wild peas and onions, the children played at taking scalps and counting coups. But behind it all was a growing sense of panic and hopelessness. Where were the sacred Medicine Arrows? Many believed the end was at hand—and that

Touch the Sky had brought this destruction to the tribe.

One sleep.

Her desperate urgency scattered all other thoughts but that of Touch the Sky. She had meant what she told Black Elk recently: If Touch the Sky were killed, she would find some way to kill Wolf Who Hunts Smiling and any others involved in the sordid scheme. She had no fear of whatever Black Elk was planning against her— except the fear that she might die before avenging her tall brave, the one true love of her young life. A man she might be living with now had fate not marked him out for a hard destiny.

Was he still alive? Where was he? He had known nothing but trouble ever since joining the tribe. And now, with Arrow Keeper gone, she had no sympathetic ear to confide in. Even her aunt, Sharp Nosed Woman, who once had harbored secret admiration for the tall youth's courage, had turned her heart against him.

By now the elk steak was sizzling, dripping melted kidney fat just the way Black Elk liked it. Honey Eater turned it, fighting back hot tears as the thought again intruded itself like an urgent drumbeat:

One sleep.

"One sleep," Wolf Who Hunts Smiling said. "One sleep, and he has run his tether out. You must not show the white feather now, this close to the blooding."

Sis-ki-dee frowned, a rare sign of annoyance replacing the usual crazy-brave grin. The four of them sat around a council fire smoking good tobacco: Wolf Who Hunts Smiling, Medicine Flute, Sis-ki-dee, and Takes His Share.

"Cheyenne, be warned. You are alive only because I have found it amusing to stay my men's hand. Speak once again about Sis-ki-dee showing the white feather, and I will have them flay your soles. Then you will be sent back to the Powder on foot."

He looked at the other Cheyenne. "As for this sleepy-eyed worm larva, if he puts that bone in his mouth one more time he will have to swallow it."

Medicine Flute hastily put his flute away after this threat. But Wolf Who Hunts Smiling felt a murderous bile erupt up his throat. This Blackfoot dog sat on Cheyenne land and spoke with the same masterly, arrogant tone of the whiteskins. Still, the men in his Panther Clan took great pride in not letting any feeling show in their faces.

"No need to rise on your hind legs, Contrary Warrior. I was not insulting your courage. Sis-ki-dee would face down the Wendigo himself, as would I. I only meant that this is no time to be discouraged. You have frustrated him thus far."

"I have, wily Wolf Who Hunts Smiling. But this battle last night cost me more braves killed and wounded. And now the Ghost Warrior has gained the mountain. Even now he is watching this camp."

"Have you flushed him?"

"Would *you* flush that one?"

Wolf Who Hunts Smiling conceded this with a nod. "You speak straight. I might flush out a silvertip bear first. But only think. If he killed more of your men, all the more reason to fasten your courage to the sticking-place. White Man Runs Him swore an oath before council. If those Arrows are not returned in one more sleep, he must submit to death."

Now Medicine Flute spoke up.

"Count upon it. I despise him as much as Wolf Who Hunts Smiling does. But certainly he is no coward. Nor would this licker of white crotches ever break his word. He has promised the tribe his own death. He will make good on that promise."

Sis-ki-dee's smallpox-scarred visage creased in another ugly frown.

"That he will keep his word is not at issue. Like most fools he places great value on the importance of a promise. The issue before us now is his skill as a warrior. Have you seen those cliffs he and his men climbed? I showed you the battlefield, the spent casings. These are willful Indians."

"They are Cheyennes."

Angrily, Sis-ki-dee gestured around them.

"Never mind your foolish pride in your tribe! Look at this ruined camp! My braves have been tempered in hard fights against blue-bloused soldiers and fierce mountain Utes. Yet this tall Cheyenne led a mere handful of warriors past us. Do you think he plans to stay in hiding like a turtle ducking into its shell?"

"Of course not. He will make his move. Only, tell me a thing. You once laughed when I warned you this brave was trouble. Now I see you frowning. Is the Red Peril, too, coming unstrung as all the rest did before they died?"

Sis-ki-dee saw the clear challenge to his courage. His evil and crazy-brave grin was back.

"You are right, this is no time to recite his coups. Only think. I and my men have wounded two of his men, perhaps seriously. Another is dead. That leaves only one healthy warrior besides him."

"I have ears for this," Wolf Who Hunts Smiling said. "This Touch the Sky, he is not a god."

"No, you are right. He walks the earth and has blood in his veins, for I have spilled it. But if a thing cuts wood, you may call it an axe. This brave certainly has the look of a god."

"A battle god," Wolf Who Hunts Smiling conceded with a nod. "But he will die if we both refuse to lose heart. As you say, he is probably watching us at this very moment. Would I allow him to see me here with you if I believed he would survive?"

Here Sis-ki-dee met his visitor's eye frankly.

"On this last point, I am curious. Knowing how dangerous it is, why have you risked another trip up here?"

Wolf Who Hunts Smiling glanced briefly at Medicine Flute before answering. *Look sharp!*

Here comes the dangerous stretch of the trail, that glance said.

"Because," he replied, "I have thought of a better plan than the one we agreed on."

Now it was Sis-ki-dee's turn to cast a sly glance at Takes His Share.

"Oh? And what is wrong with the plan we have already agreed on? Do you mean that we should *not* kill the tall dog?"

"Of course we will kill him. We both want that. That part remains unchanged. But only think, Contrary Warrior. As you have assured me, our Medicine Arrows mean nothing to you. Your only wish is to see the head of White Man Runs Him balanced on a stick. Do my words fly straight?"

Sis-ki-dee only nodded vaguely, waiting to hear more.

"Therefore," Wolf Who Hunts Smiling said, "we have come to suggest a change. Rather than returning the Arrows yourself, give them to us."

Sis-ki-dee's eyebrows shot up. His playful mood was returning now that the game was getting crafty again.

"Give them to you? There is a curious notion. Why should I do this thing?"

"Quite simple," Wolf Who Hunts Smiling said. "Our goal is to gain dominion over this territory, agreed?"

Again Sis-ki-dee nodded, but vaguely.

"That goal is best accomplished if my shaman here, Medicine Flute, receives credit for returning the Arrows. The Headmen would be turned into fawning dogs licking his hand."

"Indeed," Sis-ki-dee said contemptuously, thinking of his own tribe's headmen, "they are squaw men moved by such considerations. This would be a fine thing—for you."

"And you, buck! For we are together in this venture. What strengthens my hand also strengthens yours."

"Perhaps," Sis-ki-dee said. "Perhaps not. Never forget, I have seen how aptly you are named. A wolf who smiles while it is hunting is a dangerous beast indeed to trust."

"Granted, as is a man who calls himself the Contrary Warrior. I do not claim to be an honorable man of my word. Neither are you, and thus we can respect each other. Women and old men are 'honorable' only because they lack the strength and killing instinct to live like the eagles who boldly devour the lambs.

"But Contrary Warrior, only think on this! Even a wolf will honor an alliance that behooves his own interest. I need a brave of your cunning and strength, a brave whose thoughts fly on the same ambitious winds as mine."

Wolf Who Hunts Smiling had always prided himself on his persuasive speaking abilities. Now, as he watched the favorable impression his words created, he felt a tug of inner satisfaction.

Sis-ki-dee said, "Well spoken, Cheyenne. And I, too, can use a capable ally."

"Then you will give me the Arrows?"

"What? Now, buck?"

"Of course. It is a long ride to this place."

A grin played at Sis-ki-dee's lips.

"But wily wolf! The Noble Red Man is not yet sent under. I cannot risk returning those Arrows until he is."

"This is foolish. No one will know I have those Arrows. Nor will they until Woman Face has been separated from his head."

"I will not risk that," Sis-ki-dee insisted. "Those Arrows remain with me until the tall one's head is tendered in payment, just as we agreed."

Wolf Who Hunts Smiling watched the other closely now as he said, "May we look at the Arrows?"

If Sis-ki-dee was nonplussed by this, he hid it well.

"What? With him watching? Have you been wandering in the sun too long?"

"Very well, if there's nothing else for it. Why push when a thing won't move?"

Secretly, Wolf Who Hunts Smiling had expected just such a response. For he had guessed by now that Sis-ki-dee planned to doublecross him and either destroy those Arrows or hold them for additional ransom. But it had been necessary to go through this sham to keep up appearances. For truly, if Sis-ki-dee knew that he knew, he would kill both of them as casually as he might swat a fly.

So that's the way it is, Wolf Who Hunts Smiling thought. He would have to wait in hiding, work quickly, and somehow get those Arrows himself.

"As you say, Red Peril," Wolf Who Hunts Smiling said. "We will wait until Woman Face is worm fodder. After all, the important thing is that you do intend to return the Arrows."

Sis-ki-dee nodded, fighting back a smirk.

"Of course. What use have I for your pretty sticks?"

Chapter Twelve

Fortunately for Touch the Sky's small and battered band of warriors, the Blackfoot renegades had been left shaken by the Cheyennes' fighting spirit.

Filled with a new respect, they decided the best plan was to fort up and protect their camp. The only protection against such fighters, they agreed, was numbers. Had they risked dividing up into search parties, they might have flushed out the Cheyenne hiding place in a small, cup-shaped hollow almost within shouting distance of the camp.

"There is all the proof needed of his treachery," Tangle Hair said bitterly. "How I wish I could hear their words."

He, Touch the Sky, Little Horse, and young

Two Twists were well hidden behind a dense
spruce copse. From here they spied on the
meeting between the two Blackfoot renegades
and the two Cheyenne visitors. They had made
soft beds of young boughs for the two wounded
Cheyennes. Little Horse had been fortunate: the
slug had passed through his shoulder and left
a clean wound. Touch the Sky had packed it
with gunpowder and balsam before wrapping
it again.

Tangle Hair had not been so lucky. Touch the
Sky and Two Twists had been forced to dig the
slug out of the meaty portion of his thigh while
Tangle Hair bit down hard on a strip of rawhide.
The wound needed to be cauterized, but they
could not risk a fire. So they settled for carefully
wrapping it now.

Both men were weak, but Touch the Sky knew
they were tough enough to survive. Unfortunately,
further combat was out of the question for either
until they rested and recovered some strength.

And this was hardly the place for resting. Touch the Sky knew they risked dis-
covery at any time. Nor was all the danger
posed by humans. He had noticed how the
trees all around this spot had been clawed
high up—the territorial markings of a grizzly. This was a place to leave as soon as
possible.

As was this entire mountain.

But for now all of them could see Wolf
Who Hunts Smiling and Medicine Flute in the

Blackfoot camp, counciling with the murdering dog Sis-ki-dee.

"Where are the Arrows?" Two Twists said again. "They have parleyed for a long time now. But no sign of the Arrows. What, are they trading their clan histories?"

His voice was tense with frustration. Like the others, he felt powerless to help—powerless to help his tribe secure their Arrows, powerless to help Touch the Sky, a warrior's warrior whom Two Twists admired to the very core of his being. Who had rallied Two Twists and the other junior warriors to a brilliant defense when Kiowas and Comanches had attempted to steal their women and children during the annual hunt? Two Twists had watched Touch the Sky, who stood all alone in the open, use himself as a human lure to draw the enemy into effective range. With bullets creasing his ears and fanning his locks, he had stood tall and defiant and never once flinched, all for the sake of his tribe.

"Where are the Arrows? I know not, little brother," Touch the Sky finally replied. "Better to ask me where the buffalo go to die. But we must watch for our clue. For as surely as my blood is red, our Arrows are in that camp."

Touch the Sky gave the entire area a sweeping gaze before adding, "Or somewhere near it."

"What is the meaning of this third painting?" Little Horse said from his bed of boughs. The brave was paler than normal from blood loss. He had been studying the pictograph Arrow Keeper had left behind, unable to see much in the old shaman's crude artwork.

"Divine that answer," Touch the Sky replied, "and this trail takes a new turn. Believe me, bucks, I have studied it hard and long."

"It could be many things," Little Horse said. "It is only a long, curving line."

"Many things," Two Twists agreed. "A path?"

"Perhaps a river?"

"Could it be a snake?"

"It could be all or any of those," Touch the Sky told his friends. "But I have shed brain sweat on this matter. Think how this mountain is hollow in places from underground springs and other openings. This painting could also indicate a cave or perhaps a tunnel."

Little Horse nodded.

"You may be right, brother. Yes, you just might be. But what of that? I have noticed no tunnel or cave entrance, though truly, we have hardly had a good chance to explore this place."

"Nor are we likely to get one," Touch the Sky said. "So we must take turns watching them constantly, especially Sis-ki-dee. If he—"

"Brothers!" Two Twists cut in. "Look! Wolf Who Hunts Smiling and Medicine Flute are leaving."

"So it would appear," Touch the Sky said, watching the two braves head toward the slope and their waiting ponies. "We dare not break cover to follow them, and we cannot spare a man anyway. Only two of us are able. Let us hope they are truly returning to the Powder River camp, not going to the place where the Arrows are hidden."

One sleep, he thought desperately. With sunset tomorrow, he must either surrender himself for execution or bear the responsibility for ruining his tribe—as well as breaking an oath made before council. Keeping his word was doubly hard because he knew that Sis-ki-dee would never keep his.

If all that weren't trouble enough for one brave's lifetime, there was more. His death would also mark Honey Eater out for some awful fate. Arrow Keeper had predicted these things, and not once had Touch the Sky known him to err concerning medicine visions.

But for now, exhaustion had him and Two Twists firmly in its grip. He looked at the youth's face. It had aged ten years since beginning that harrowing climb up the northern face of this bad-medicine mountain. And truly, when had the tough little brave last slept?

"Two Twists?"

"I have ears."

"And a stout heart, buck," Touch the Sky told him. "With braves like you surrounding him, a man could sleep in peace at night. And speaking of sleep, lie down now. Then I will do the same while you watch."

Two Twists was too exhausted to protest. He was dead to the world almost as soon as he closed his eyes.

Fighting back stone-heavy eyelids and dizzying

waves of exhaustion, Touch the Sky constantly monitored the camp below. Secure in their concentrated numbers, the Blackfoot marauders had not bothered to establish an outlying guard.

He watched them amuse themselves by gambling, running foot races through the camp, wrestling, drinking the cheap whiskey sold illegally to Indians at the trading post at Red Shale. Many lined up to arm-wrestle between circles of hot coals, the loser receiving a harsh burn when his strength gave out. But Sis-ki-dee went inside of his hide-covered lodge and spent most of his time there. Several times Touch the Sky saw him step outside to scan the surrounding area thoughtfully—much as the Cheyenne himself was doing.

Finally, black waves of weariness washing over his depleted body, Touch the Sky woke Two Twists. The two wounded braves had both slipped into a fitful sleep.

"Watch carefully, little brother, while I join our comrades. If you see any sign of our Arrows, wake me."

Two Twists nodded. His eyes lifted upward to the heavens, tracking the progress of Sister Sun. She was almost straight overhead now. Time was slipping away from them like water running through their fingers.

He met Touch the Sky's eyes and nodded. Like well-trained Cheyenne warriors, both braves kept their fear out of their faces. But their eyes said it clearly without words: *We are up against it now.*

May Maiyun help our tribe, and soon, or Gray Thunder's Shaiyena people will be in a hurting place.

Touch the Sky's last thought, as he tumbled down into blessed sleep, was of old Arrow Keeper.

That, and the vague awareness of a sound further up the mountain: the triumphant kill cry of a mountain lion.

He dreamed, but not just one dream. It was as if the entire, tumultuous history of his life was paraded before his mind's eye in fleeting images.

He saw Bighorn Falls, the sleepy river-bend town where he had grown up as Matthew Hanchon with his adopted white parents; Kristin Steele, her bottomless blue eyes smiling at him as they met in their secret copse; the long-jawed, malicious face of her father's wrangler, Boone Wilson, as he beat the 16-year-old senseless for daring to love a white woman.

He saw himself riding out alone from Bighorn Falls in the dead of night, bridle pointed toward Cheyenne country, after Lt. Seth Carlson's threat to ruin his parents' mercantile business if he remained in town. Then came images of all his struggles and battles as a Cheyenne: images of torture by fire and near-starvation and festering wounds and ferocious combat.

All of it was familiar, a dream litany of his

hard life as a warrior caught between two worlds, welcome in neither.

And then came the one brief image that didn't fit, that made no apparent sense. The ridiculous image of Arrow Keeper.

The old shaman was completely naked, a younger man now though clearly Arrow Keeper. He was riding down a steep mountainside, long hair streaming out behind him in the wind.

Only, he wasn't riding a pony—he was mounted on the back of a magnificent mountain lion!

Brother.
Wake up, brother.
Touch the Sky!

"Wake up!" Two Twists repeated urgently, giving Touch the Sky a hard shake.

Abruptly the tall warrior sat up.

"What is it?"

Sister Sun had tracked even further west. A deep, luminous gold sheen lay over Wendigo Mountain.

"Look," Two Twists said, pointing. "Sis-ki-dee has headed up toward the peak by himself."

Touch the Sky looked where the youth pointed. He watched the Blackfoot leader swing wide around a spot where a patch of trees had been obliterated by a rock slide. He was indeed picking his way toward the peak. For a moment the sun glinted off his brassards and the huge brass rings dangling from his ears.

Then Touch the Sky spotted something else,

and his pulse suddenly quickened.

It was a brief glimpse of a tawny hide streaking up toward the remote pinnacle. A mountain lion. Alerted by his strange vision, Touch the Sky knew this was no coincidence.

He watched the lion bound higher and higher before seeming to disappear suddenly near the peak. He was just able to distinguish a slight cleft in the gray expanse of rock—no doubt the entrance to its den.

No, this was no coincidence. Old Arrow Keeper was still protecting the Sacred Arrows. In the face of utter hopelessness, he had sent this vision as a goad to his young assistant's flagging determination.

"Look!" Two Twists said. "Sis-ki-dee has stopped again. What is he doing?"

Two Twists had not noticed the mountain lion. But Touch the Sky had seen Sis-ki-dee watching it. And now the Contrary Warrior abruptly turned around again and returned to his camp.

"Bucks," Touch the Sky said, for the other two Cheyennes were awake now, too. "I believe we have located the Medicine Arrows!"

The rest stared at him expectantly, waiting for more. But there was no time now for explanations.

"Wait here," he told Two Twists. When the youth started to object, he added, "It will be difficult enough for one man to remain hidden, let alone two. Do not feel slighted, young buck. You may yet get another ration of hard fighting, if your belly hungers for it. For now, banish all thoughts of glory and think only of the need to find those Arrows."

It was a dangerous journey, and with every heartbeat Touch the Sky expected shots to ring out.

Fixing the exact location of the den in his mind, Touch the Sky broke from cover and headed up. The most direct route, unfortunately, cut through the Blackfoot camp. Touch the Sky was forced to swing wide to the west to avoid it, then double back.

Even so, he was dangerously exposed when he raced from boulder to boulder, from stunted tree to the next low-lying swale. There was not enough time to do this thing correctly, an advance that, by rights, should have taken a better part of the day.

He kept a wary eye on the camp. But so far Sis-ki-dee had not come out again. Soon Touch the Sky had slipped close enough to hear the mewling of young lion cubs coming from just inside the cleft in the rocks. This area was well disguised from below, a rockslide having caused a massive deadfall of trees that served as a blind.

He stayed downwind from the den. A mountain lion with young to protect would be a formidable foe indeed. Touch the Sky knew it was foolish to attempt to get any closer. He had his Sharps to hand, a round behind the loading gate. But one shot would bring that entire camp swarming over him.

Impatiently, he settled behind a boulder and waited. Soon the hungry mother rewarded him by slipping back outside again. She was already stalking more food to strengthen her milk for the cubs.

Touch the Sky waited until she had disappeared behind a razorback ridge to the east. Then, moving quickly forward in a crouch, he made it to the entrance and slipped inside the lion's den.

Chapter Thirteen

"I saw the she-bitch return a short time ago," Sis-ki-dee told Takes His Share. "So I turned back. I have no desire to kill such a valuable ally. But I have watched her habits closely. By now she will have gone back out to hunt. I am returning to her den."

The two Blackfoot renegades stood in the center of their now heavily guarded camp. Sentries along the southern slope would signal long before any surprise attack by additional braves from the Powder River camp would stand a chance.

The only risk, to Sis-ki-dee's mind, was that tall Ghost Warrior and his band.

"They are close," Sis-ki-dee told Takes His Share again. "Never doubt that. For there sinks the sun, sinking too the tall buck's chances as well as any

hope for his tribe. Their boldness will increase
with their desperation."

"My thoughts too, Contrary Warrior. Have I
ever spoken any way but one about this Cheyenne
devil? I fear him and freely admit it. Only. . . ."

Sis-ki-dee tossed back his cropped head and
laughed.

" 'Only' what? Do not play the coy woman, buck!
Spit your words out as if you have a set on you!
Say it bold, what troubles you?"

"Only this. As you say, they are watching our
camp. So why, having stopped them this long,
reveal the hiding place of the Arrows now?"

"Because, buck, I plan to reveal more than
the hiding place. I mean to reveal the Arrows
to them."

Takes His Share gaped stupidly. "But, Sis-ki-
dee, for what good reason?"

"Am I ever without a good reason, even when it
is not always immediately clear? Did we not just
agree that the Cheyennes' boldness will increase
with their desperation?"

Takes His Share nodded. He watched his war
leader check the load in his North and Savage.
Then Sis-ki-dee slid the Bowie from its sheath
and tested the edge with a thumb.

"And how many sleeps remain before they run
out of time?"

"Only one."

"Only one, indeed," Sis-ki-dee agreed. "And
soon, we are plunged into darkness when the
sun goes down. Better if they make their move

while we can see them. Even more important, *I* want to control this thing. Sis-ki-dee is no brave to sit in his tipi, waiting patiently, until he is called out to the fight."

Sis-ki-dee's eyes glinted as they narrowed to study the surrounding terrain. For several heartbeats they focused thoughtfully on the narrow entrance to the lion's den, a mere dark line against the blight caused by the rockslide.

"They are out there, buck. So I will fetch those Arrows into plain view now as a lure and a reminder. This Cheyenne blister has chafed at us long enough. Now it is time to pop it once and for all.

"Keep a close eye on things down here," he added.

A moment later he started up through the huge piles of scree, angling toward the mountain lion's den.

Touch the Sky paid scant attention to the mewling and whimpering of the cubs, squirming balls of fur in their soft bed to the left of the entrance. But he reminded himself to hurry. Few animals were more ferocious than a mountain lion protecting her young. And he had no idea how far away this one's hunting territory extended.

Fortunately, enough light remained to illuminate the cavern chamber. A quick, cursory look revealed nothing. But he hadn't really expected it to—Sis-ki-dee was not that careless.

Trying to quell the urgency inside him, Touch

the Sky began a more thorough search of the chamber. Occasionally, at first, he hurried to the entrance and glanced outside to make sure that nothing—on two legs or four—was approaching. But as he became more absorbed in searching the farther reaches of the stone cavern, he neglected to check as often.

He peered into every nook and cranny; he slipped his fingers into every cleft; he probed every possible opening. He felt the uneven rock floor for hiding places, ran his eye carefully overhead.

Nothing.

The desperation welled up inside him, but he fought it down the way a man overcomes a temptation. Desperation led to panic, and panic left a warrior useless. He thought of Arrow Keeper, and that thought calmed him.

He was sure now that the old shaman was with him, helping him even now, if only he could clear his mind and attend closer to his shaman senses. Had not the pictograph already proven valuable? Had Arrow Keeper not sent him medicine visions as clues?

Touch the Sky knew he had not ended up here purely by chance. The hand of the Good Supernatural—with Arrow Keeper's assistance—had guided him to this place. And those Arrows were close. He could feel the weight of their presence as a person can feel the weight of a hidden stare.

As the twig is bent, so the tree shall grow, the old

medicine man had told him long ago. This was during his first initiation into the Cheyenne way. And thanks in part to Arrow Keeper's wisdom, had this tree called Touch the Sky not grown straight and tall and strong? A tree to match its lofty name?

Deliberately, Touch the Sky brought his rapid, uneven breathing under calm control.

He willed his tense muscles to relax.

Despite the danger pressing in on him from all sides, he cleared his mind of all fear, of all 'thought.' He stood there in the center of the cavern, his eyes closed, his mind free but attentive.

Outside, the winds lashing Wendigo Mountain rose to a hollow, shrieking cry that sounded unmistakably human, the voices of those long-ago Cheyenne hunters whose souls were trapped in this most unholy of places. But Touch the Sky refused to let fear violate his quiet, motionless concentration.

The knowledge came to him all at once, certain and sure and beyond language. When he finally stirred himself again, his movements were sure and precise. He knew right where to go, the way beavers know where to build their dams.

Touch the Sky crossed to the back of the big chamber. He stepped behind an abutment of limestone and into the well-concealed tunnel he had missed the first time around. Several overhead airshafts sent light stabbing into the sunken tunnel.

Looking due north, Touch the Sky could see

that this was only one of a maze of several tunnels. They slanted down toward the cliffs at the backside of Wendigo Mountain. He wanted to explore them. But for now he was concerned with one spot just past the entrance of this first tunnel.

He propped his Sharps against the damp stone wall. Then, hand over hand, he climbed to the top of the tunnel and thrust one hand up into a narrow space near the cold stone ceiling.

He probed a fissure, and immediately his fingers brushed slick oilskin.

Elated, heart stomping against his ribs, Touch the Sky climbed quickly back down and stepped into a shaft of light. Carefully setting the bundle down, he knelt beside it. Heart hammering with apprehension and anticipation, he opened the slicker.

Fingers trembling, he opened the soft coyote-fur pouch inside. Then his grim lips eased into a wide smile—the first that had touched his face for some time.

There lay all four Medicine Arrows, sweet and clean as he was sworn to keep them.

Quickly, all business now, he wrapped the Arrows in their fur pouch again, then folded the slicker around them. He had just begun to stow them away when an angry snarl behind him turned his blood to ice.

Touch the Sky whirled and spotted his rifle, too far away to be any help now. But it would have been useless even if he had held it in his hands, because the very moment he turned to look behind him, the enraged mountain lion slammed into him like a blurry yellow missile and knocked him flat.

"Panther Clan, this scheme would be scanned," Medicine Flute said nervously. "This Sis-ki-dee is no brave to trifle with."

"Truer notes never crossed your lips, flute blower," Wolf Who Hunts Smiling replied. "He is no brave to trifle with, indeed. That is why we are here."

The wily Cheyenne nodded toward the Colt Model 1855 percussion rifle in his hands. It had been among the possessions stripped from Touch the Sky when he was still called Matthew Hanchon and wore white man's shoes. By now it had seen hard service. A strip of buckskin reinforced the cracked stock.

"I have no plans to trifle with him. I see now that it is useless to attempt sharing power with that one. I mean to get those Arrows and then kill him. Nothing trifling in that."

After failing, during his recent meeting with the Blackfoot, to secure the Medicine Arrows, Wolf Who Hunts Smiling decided on a bold and decisive plan of action. Instead of returning to their camp, he and Medicine Flute took up a position in a thicket to the south.

Clearly, the Cheyenne now realized, he had been a fool to give those Arrows to Sis-ki-dee. Once they were actually in his hands, Wolf Who

Hunts Smiling had nearly panicked. If his tribe ever caught him with them, no amount of sly talk would save him from a hard death. Thus he had shown bad judgment in trusting the Blackfoot renegade.

Now it only remained to figure out where those Arrows were hidden. Wolf Who Hunts Smiling had received his first valuable clue when Sis-ki-dee had started up toward that peak, then halted when he spotted the mountain lion.

Wolf Who Hunts Smiling couldn't see, from this altitude and angle, the precise spot where the she-bitch actually entered her den. Nor could he see very far west of this low-lying position— the direction from which Touch the Sky and the lion had approached and entered the den.

But he could clearly now see Sis-ki-dee starting back up toward the peak again. And a further stroke of luck: the braves in camp, bored by their constant vigilance, were placing bets on target plinking. One more shot might not be noticed among all the shots already echoing atop the mountain.

"Now we are close to owning the Arrows, buck," he assured Medicine Flute. "Sis-ki-dee is not climbing up there to relieve himself. If you know how to fire that rusted firestick of yours, be ready. For I am about to stir things up around here."

With that, Wolf Who Hunts Smiling broke from cover and made his way closer to the pinnacle of Wendigo Mountain.

*   *   *

The mountain lion leaped on Touch the Sky so hard that the impact brought him down immediately.

He felt the sudden animal warmth of the contact, stared directly into those slavering jaws, felt fire erupt in his side as several claws raked bloody furrows. Gobbets of fresh meat still clung to the cat's deadly fangs.

The lithe killer had gone straight for his jugular. But the momentum of its powerful leap made it overshoot its human mark, claws raking on the stone behind him as the lion hit hard and quickly recovered for another leap.

But the delay gave Touch the Sky just enough time to snatch his obsidian knife from its sheath. He rolled hard to the right as the lion leaped again, missing him by inches.

The Cheyenne rose to his knees, then into a low squat. Powerful leg muscles bunching, he leaped on the cat.

The lion was an eyeblink quicker, managing to scuttle just enough to avert the killing blow; it was turned to a wound instead as the blade caught the cat just above the right forepaw.

A snarl of rage, an unbelievably fast spin, and the lion was on Touch the Sky.

The youth managed to get an arm up, protecting his face from the deadly fangs. He arched his back hard, tossing the cat. In a heartbeat it was up again and flying at him.

Once more molten fire poured over him as

the sharp claws ripped into his chest. But this time Touch the Sky managed one good thrust of his knife. The blade caught the lion in the soft underfold of its belly.

Desperate, knowing another wound would never stop this blood-lusting beast, Touch the Sky drove his knife clear to the hilt, then gave it the 'Spanish twist,' ripping deep and wide into warm vitals. He felt heat escape from the lion's punctured organs, felt the huge beast quiver violently, then unleash a fierce death cry. Finally it went slack, its wild blood mingled with the Cheyenne's.

For a moment Touch the Sky lay gasping under the dead beast, chest heaving as he got his breath back. Then, sore muscles protesting the effort, he threw the dead animal off him and staggered to his feet.

Touch the Sky limped across to the spot where he had left the Arrows. He gave silent thanks to Maiyun when he realized they had remained unscathed throughout his desperate struggle with the mountain lion.

"I did not choose to violate your home and leave your children orphans, cousin," he said quietly and with genuine regret at having been forced to kill this animal. After all, she had only been defending her young.

Below, in the camp, he heard the drunken cheers, the guns going off as the wild braves shot at targets. He was about to pick up the Arrows when a familiar laugh made his skin crawl.

"The Noble Red Man braves all to save his tribe's pretty-painted sticks! Then he cries over a dead lion. Better to cry for his own hide, for truly his days between the sky and the earth are now over!"

Touch the Sky whirled. Sis-ki-dee filled the opening of the den. The sun backlighted him in a bloody penumbra. His finger slid inside the trigger guard of his big North and Savage rifle.

"My mistake has been in always insisting on taking you alive. Each time you managed to somehow play the fox."

"Perhaps," Touch the Sky replied, merely sparring for time, "you are not so clever as you think."

"Perhaps not. But here I stand, rifle trained on you. And over there is your weapon. Use magic, shaman, and cause it to fly into your hands."

Suddenly Touch the Sky focused his eyes behind Sis-ki-dee, as if someone had appeared in the entrance behind him.

Sis-ki-dee laughed. "Truly, you are a game bird! Even now you pull tricks out of your parfleche."

With no warning, the mirth bled from Sis-ki-dee's face. His finger took up the trigger slack.

"Never mind skinning off your face while you are still alive to see it," he said. "It will impress my men just as much after you are dead."

Sis-ki-dee caressed the trigger.

"Take your last breath, Ghost Warrior! Sis-ki-dee never misses at this range. Nor will you turn this bullet to sand. It does not matter how loudly you sing your death song. This is Wendigo Mountain. Any Cheyenne who dies here dies unclean!"

Chapter Fourteen

Sis-ki-dee's last word still hung in the air, mocking Touch the Sky on the threshold of death, when a rifle shot sounded above the moaning of the wind. But Touch the Sky knew that a man never hears the shot that kills him—*this* bullet wasn't meant to send him over.

Even as his battle-savvy brain registered this fact, he watched a round rip through Sis-ki-dee's leather shirt. It had been fired by someone outside the entrance to the den. Had Two Twists disobeyed orders, Touch the Sky wondered, and broken from cover?

Touch the Sky gave thanks for insubordinate junior warriors, for evidently Two Twists had just saved his life. But all this flashed through the Cheyenne's mind in an eyeblink. Even as his brain grappled with events, his body sprang into action.

Sis-ki-dee had leaped to the floor upon feeling the tug of a bullet rip through his shirt. Certain he was being attacked by the rest of the Cheyennes, he scrambled to his feet and lunged toward the secret escape tunnels. His rifle came up to the ready as he charged at the Cheyenne intruder.

Instinctively, Touch the Sky's first move was to scoop up the Sacred Arrows. Sis-ki-dee was rising as he leaped over the dead mountain lion. Touch the Sky lunged for his Sharps, still propped against the wall of the cavern. He only had time to swing the rifle up and snap off a round without aiming.

He missed. Luckily, so did Sis-ki-dee. But the Blackfoot's round struck rock only inches from Touch the Sky's eyes and flung powder into them, temporarily blinding him.

Reflexively, Touch the Sky dropped the oilskin pouch as his hand flew to his eyes. By the time he could open them again, blurry now with tears, he saw Sis-ki-dee disappearing around an elbow turn in the main tunnel—and the yellow oilskin was clutched close to his side!

It was not Two Twists who fired the bullet that saved Touch the Sky's life.

Unaware that he was in fact saving his worst enemy in the world, Wolf Who Hunts Smiling had only meant to kill this renegade Blackfoot who meant to play the fox with him. For surely the Arrows were inside that den. And Wolf Who Hunts Smiling wanted to seize this moment for the kill, when a volley of shots from camp covered the noise of his own shot.

But in his eager haste he had felt himself jerk his trigger at the last moment, throwing off his aim.

Had he at least wounded the Blackfoot? It was hard to tell from here. But shots had been fired inside the cave, too. Hope welled inside Wolf Who Hunts Smiling. Had one of those shots, fired after his own, finally snuffed the life of White Man Runs Him?

Now he quickly reloaded. Staying out of sight of those below, he scrambled up toward that entrance. He avoided the great golden splashes of light made by the day's late sunlight.

He must lay hands on those Arrows! Never mind whether or not they meant anything spiritually. With them safely stored in Medicine Flute's tipi, Wolf Who Hunts Smiling would bend the people to his own purposes. Soon would begin a great war of extermination against all the whiteskin invaders.

But even now, caught flush in the excitement of danger, two questions nagged at him: Where was Sis-ki-dee, and where was Touch the Sky?

As Sis-ki-dee disappeared from view, his insane, mocking laughter taunted Touch the Sky and dared him to follow.

Wendigo Mountain

Follow the Cheyenne did, although this maze of tunnels was unfamiliar to him. Just enough light filtered down through the airshafts to illuminate the tunnels in a grainy sort of twilight.

First he paused to reload. Going mostly by touch in the stingy light, he fished a paper cartridge from his parfleche. He chewed off one end, shook the powder into his charger, seated the ball. Then he thumbed a primer cap behind the loading gate.

When he'd finished, Touch the Sky stood stone silent, stone still, and listened.

The noises from camp receded behind him now, but not the mournful howling of the wind. It chased itself in and out of the numerous airshafts, reminding Touch the Sky of the noise the wind used to make in the stovepipes back at his childhood home in Bighorn Falls.

Beyond the mournful sound of the wind, he heard something else: faint footsteps, moving out ahead of him. He started toward them, but soon he halted. His brow wrinkled in confusion.

For now the footsteps seemed to come from his right. He took the next tunnel that jogged in that direction. But as soon as he did so, the noise of someone running seemed to shift to his left.

Again Touch the Sky stopped, confused and disoriented.

Then, clear as a rattler's warning in still morning air, he heard it: Sis-ki-dee's high-pitched, insane, mocking laughter. Much closer than he expected.

And then a pebble bounced off his back, and Touch the Sky flinched violently. He whirled and drew a bead—on empty air.

The crazy laughter rose an octave, blending into the steady shriek of the wind.

Takes His Share grew impatient.

The Contrary Warrior had told him to keep an eye on things. But only Sis-ki-dee could truly control these braves when they were becoming wild. And now, as the liquor flowed, they were indeed wild.

A group, faces flushed with drunkenness, had gathered around a campfire. Now they tossed cartridges into the flames and waited for the round to detonate, risking their lives merely for the thrill of it. If Sis-ki-dee was gone much longer, there wouldn't be any camp to return to.

Takes His Share slipped his big-bore Lancaster under his arm and headed up the slope. The last of the day's sun blazed in its full glory now, throwing the Sans Arcs peaks into dark silhouette.

He picked his way carefully across the blighted area caused by the rockslide, his rifle at the ready in case the cat was inside. Then he stuck his head into the narrow cleft.

"Contrary Warrior? Are you in there? Can you hear me?"

Nothing. But he thought he heard a faint noise within.

Cautiously he stuck his head inside.

Cold steel kissed his temple, and then a bright

explosion of orange sent Takes His Share across when Wolf Who Hunts Smiling blew his brains all over the rock wall beside him.

"I know what he said," Two Twists said impatiently to Little Horse. "But he has been gone far too long now."

Little Horse winced as he rolled to a sitting position and glanced up the slope in the direction Touch the Sky had gone.

"I agree, little brother. But let me go."

"You! Here, aim this."

The younger brave handed his British trade rifle to Little Horse. But his left arm had stiffened so badly he could not even lift it to aim.

"See? Tangle Hair cannot walk, and you cannot shoot. It comes down to me. If it were up to you, you would have gone to check on Touch the Sky by now."

Little Horse was forced to nod at this.

"Then go. But move carefully, buck, and keep an eye on your back-trail. Hear them in that camp? If they catch you, count upon it, your screams will provide the night's entertainment."

Two Twists nodded, nervous sweat beading on his upper lip. Holding his rifle at a high port, he moved out through the piles of scree.

Wolf Who Hunts Smiling could not puzzle this situation out.

He had found no blood on the rocks, so evidently his shot had missed Sis-ki-dee. And this dead lion explained the shots he had heard after his own. But where was Sis-ki-dee?

He had made a quick search of the cavern, missing the hidden tunnel entrance at the back. And then that fool Takes His Share had come sniffing after his own death.

Now what? Wolf Who Hunts Smiling had searched this entire cavern and found no sign of the Arrows. He couldn't remain here much longer. Soon someone from below would miss Sis-ki-dee or Takes His Share.

Frustrated, but knowing there was nothing else for it, he stepped over the dead Indian and left the cavern.

Deep in the maze of hidden tunnels, the deadly cat-and-mouse game went on.

Touch the Sky could not be sure if he was the pursuer or the pursued. At one moment he would hear footsteps out ahead of him. The next, he heard the steps coming up from behind him. But always, when he whirled around, there was nothing there. At least, nothing he could see in the smoky lighting.

It was a war of nerves, and no one was better than Sis-ki-dee at waging this style of fight. The Blackfoot knew these tunnels and thus had a distinct advantage over the Cheyenne. Touch the Sky had no idea, when he first had plunged into the maze, just how extensive the tunnels were.

They turned and twisted, took sharp dog-leg turns that sent him back over ground he had just covered. Occasionally, in the confusing dimness ahead, he would glimpse what he thought was a figure. When he had a clear shot, he took it. Now and then his enemy fired back, and Touch the Sky heard the protracted whine as bullets ricocheted from wall to wall along the tunnels.

"Ghost Warrior!" a voice rang out, and Touch the Sky instinctively crouched, unable to pinpoint its location.

"Ghost Warrior! I have one of your Arrows in my hand now! Listen! I am going to break your pretty stick!"

There was indeed a sharp sound of wood snapping. Touch the Sky winced as if he'd been kicked in the groin.

"Here! Stick this in your parfleche!"

Something struck the stone wall out in front of him. Touch the Sky groped ahead, stooped to feel the floor of the tunnel. His heart thumped as if he had just run hard up a long hill.

His groping fingers felt broken wood, and his heart sank.

Then he pulled it into a shaft of light and saw it was only a normal flint-tipped arrow of the type used by the Blackfoot tribe.

The mocking laughter again, seeming to come from all around him in this place without directions.

Two Twists looked just as puzzled as Wolf Who Hunts Smiling had.

He saw the dead lion, the dead Blackfoot. And

like Wolf Who Hunts Smiling, he failed to find any secret tunnel entrance at the back of this big cavern. Clearly some lively sport had taken place here. At least that was not Touch the Sky lying dead there near the entrance. Would that it were Sis-ki-dee instead of just his lieutenant.

He was about to back out of the cavern and look elsewhere when he remembered.

He remembered how he had fallen to his knees, speechless with fright, when he climbed over the cliff to confront the dead Shoots the Bear standing over them in that ghastly lightning. And he remembered his hot anger when he realized what the murdering renegades had done to Cheyenne dead.

His face grim with sudden resolution, he set his rifle aside and squatted beside the dead brave. Turnabout was fair play. He slipped both hands under the arms of the corpse and began tugging it to its feet.

Sis-ki-dee had stashed plenty of ropes at the end of the tunnels where they debouched out of the face of the cliffs. But he had no intention of making that long climb down except as a last resort. By now, any Cheyennes who had come into the cavern after him should be gone. Better to simply kill this tall dog in the tunnels, then return to the lion's den.

So far it had been child's play to track his movements. Sis-ki-dee knew all the places where he could cross to a new tunnel and thus slip behind the confused Cheyenne. True, he had not yet gotten a clear shot at him. But as soon as he did, all playing would be over.

He stopped for a moment, listening for any noises that did not belong to the wind. A smile divided his face as he heard stealthy movements just ahead, where two tunnels formed an intersection. The Ghost Warrior would have to emerge from one or the other.

He squatted back in the shadows and set the oilskin bundle down. His index finger eased inside the trigger guard and took up the slack.

Touch the Sky stopped just back from the opening ahead of him. A cool breeze licked his face and told him he was crossing another tunnel.

But his shaman sense felt something else—the familiar cool prickle of impending danger.

He moved another step closer, hugging the cool stone wall. Now he sensed the menace in the air.

Another step, and the fine hairs on his nape stood up.

He waited, took a long breath, expelled it.

Now, whispered Arrow Keeper's voice, *charge him quick while he's expecting you to crawl to your death. Now, tall warrior!*

"Hii-ya! Hii-*ya!*"

Touch the Sky leaped from the tunnel, saw his surprised quarry squatting in an adjacent tunnel, raised his Sharps, and fired. The bullet hit Sis-ki-dee square in the tough brass rings of his brassards, ricocheting off. But the tough Blackfoot renegade had the reflexes of a wolverine. In an instant he was gone, his mocking laughter taunting the Cheyenne.

Now Sis-ki-dee depended on his knowledge of the tunnels to lead his quarry a merry chase. It was run and duck and shoot as Touch the Sky chased his enemy down for the final kill. When Sis-ki-dee was sure the Cheyenne was lost deep in the bowels of the maze, he made straight for the cavern again, Medicine Arrows clutched tightly under one arm.

Outside, the sun was finally saying good-bye in a last glorious burst of flaring gold. Sis-ki-dee, chest heaving from his exertions, broke into the main cavern again. A fast glance told him no enemies were lurking about.

Then he glimpsed a figure standing near the entrance, waiting.

His rifle was instantly tucked into his shoulder socket. Then he grinned by way of greeting as he recognized the figure: It was only Takes His Share.

"Quickly, buck!" he told his lackey. "Outside the cave! I hear him coming. We'll wait for our rabbit to poke his nose out, then let daylight into his soul!"

Takes His Share said nothing, only stood there staring at him. Now Sis-ki-dee squinted in confusion. He moved closer, stared even harder. Then the bold warrior who did not believe in spirits realized with a cold shudder that was not foam coming out of Takes His Share's ear, it was his brains!

His dead companion stood in the entrance, staring at him. How could this thing be?

"No," Sis-ki-dee said, backing away as fright turned his calves to water. "I never harmed you, leave me alone!"

Now there was nothing else for it. He faced a walking dead man before him, a superb Cheyenne warrior behind. His only chance was to duck back into those tunnels and escape down the cliffs.

Caught in a bone-numbing panic, Sis-ki-dee never even noticed that he had dropped the Medicine Arrows to the floor of the cavern. Only concerned to get away from this evil spirit and the blood-lusting Cheyenne, he spun on his heel and raced back into the network of tunnels.

Chapter Fifteen

An angry but nervous Sis-ki-dee lowered himself down the precarious northern face of Wendigo Mountain, forced into a hard climb that wiped the arrogant grin from his face. Only a few stone throws away, separated from him by the rock shell of the mountain, Touch the Sky continued his fruitless search of the tunnels.

The shaman senses soon convinced him he was alone in the confusing maze. But where was Sis-ki-dee, and from which direction had he left? So far Touch the Sky had been unable to find the point where the tunnels debouched at the cliff. Perhaps he was wrong, perhaps they did not provide another way out. Maybe Sis-ki-dee had merely doubled past him in the dark maze and left by the entrance on the southern slope.

Frustrated, he worked his way back to the main chamber, mainly guided by the increased lighting at that end of the tunnel. It was nearly dark now. Wandering around would only get him killed when Sis-ki-dee returned to his camp and alerted the men—assuming he hadn't done so already. They might be grouped out there right now, rifles trained on that opening.

Thus preoccupied, Touch the Sky almost tripped over the Medicine Arrows.

He had just eased out from behind the limestone outcropping that hid the tunnel entrance. His moccasin brushed something that rustled. When he glanced down and recognized the yellow oilskin glimmering in the stingy light, his heart missed a beat.

Afraid to look closer, yet knowing he must, Touch the Sky squatted lower. He unwrapped the slicker, then the coyote fur, and peered close in the weak light. All the while his face showed nothing.

Then a wide smile eased onto his face as he realized that all four Arrows were there, all whole and all sweet and all clean.

But it seemed too easy. How did they just happen to be lying there for the taking? Where was Sis-ki-dee? Touch the Sky glanced toward the front of the chamber and, squinting in the half-light, spotted a figure waiting.

Too late his tired mind warned him: *It's a trap!*

He drew the Arrows close, about to tuck and roll back into the darkling tunnels. But then the realization struck him, more a feeling than any visual evidence: Whoever it was, he wasn't moving. And something about the perfect lack of motion told him he would never move again.

He rose, took a step closer, took a few more. Now, near the body, he recognized Sis-ki-dee's favorite. He could also see the rocks propped around the feet and ankles. And he recognized the familiar braiding pattern of the buffalo-hair rope that he could see kept the upper-body weight from falling.

The sturdy braid used by Two Twists' clan, famous for their strong ropes.

Suddenly Touch the Sky understood what must have happened to Sis-ki-dee.

Elation tingled his blood. But this was hardly a moment for celebrating. He still had to get those Arrows out of this enemy stronghold and safely back to the Powder River camp.

His face wrinkled in distaste as he cut the rope that held up Takes His Share. The dead Blackfoot slumped heavily down, and Touch the Sky stepped over him—averting his eyes in case the dead man's ghost tried to enter him that way. He ducked for cover in the same movement that brought him outside.

"Brother! Is it you? I almost shot you for Sis-ki-dee!"

"Am I that ugly, Two Twists?" He made out the shadowy mass of his young friend, ensconced in the rocks.

"Not only is it I, stout buck," he added, "but

thanks to your grisly handiwork inside, look what I carry!"

"Our Arrows!"

Even in the weak light Touch the Sky could make out the youth's wide smile.

"But how did *I* get them back?" Two Twists demanded. "I have been out here hiding, useless as a cowering rabbit."

"A rabbit, then, worth five braves! Tell me, rabbit, did Sis-ki-dee come out this way?"

"If he had, brother, either he or I would lie here dead."

Touch the Sky nodded. "As I thought. Your little puppet show with the dead scared the big Indian witless. He dropped the Arrows and ran. I would wager a new blanket that he is on the cliff even now."

"Then Maiyun grant that he be dashed to a pulp on the turrets!"

Touch the Sky nodded toward the main camp below.

"Save your oaths for later, buck. We must slip past the rest of them, and quickly. Soon the dogs will miss their master."

"But how, without ponies? Tangle Hair cannot walk, and Little Horse cannot easily climb over all the scree we must cross."

Touch the Sky watched the huge bonfires down in camp. Their tall flames threw a flickering, lurid glow over everything, distorting shapes and shadows. Though the low-lying camp was sheltered from the winds, the noise still shrieked in the air all around them.

"Their corral is past one end of camp. We could get to it quickly from here. But too many Blackfoot devils are clustered nearby. We need a diversion to clear them out."

"What type of diversion, brother? Shots fired on them?"

"No, muzzle flash would give us away."

As he spoke, Touch the Sky had been watching a lone pony that grazed, untethered, in the sporadic clumps of grass between this position and the camp below. It was a broken-down nag, obviously kept around for packwork. But such horses often became friendly with humans.

He glanced back over his shoulder toward the cave entrance where the dead Blackfoot lay.

"If it worked once, and with *him*," Touch the Sky mused out loud, "perhaps it would work again down below."

"Brother, I am slow with riddles. What do you mean?"

"You will see soon enough. For now, hie down that slope and talk sweet words to that pony. Grab its halter and lead it up here. But be careful not to show yourself."

While Two Twists did as he was told, Touch the Sky stepped back into the den and hauled the dead Blackfoot outside. By the time Two Twists showed up, leading the pony, Touch the Sky had cut the buffalo-hair rope into several shorter lengths.

"Time for this one to make one last ride,"

Touch the Sky said grimly. "Here, help me get this reluctant rider mounted. Then be ready to seize the moment, Cheyenne."

Both Cheyennes averted their nostrils when they breathed so the ghost wouldn't enter them. Once the dead man was mounted and tied into place, Two Twists dug into his parfleche.

"Wait," he said, "one more touch."

Touch the Sky let Two Twists add his macabre detail. Then he led the pony closer to the west end of camp, the end nearest the corral. When he had gone as close as he dared, he slapped the pony's rump and turned it loose.

Touch the Sky crouched behind a rock and watched. The obedient, docile mount walked slowly into the huge-glowing circle of the bonfires. At first a few men, busy drinking and cavorting, only raised a careless hand in greeting.

Then the pony stopped right beside the biggest fire.

Someone pointed, shouted something. Suddenly the rest nearby fell silent and stared at Takes His Share.

His face grinned foolishly in death. A piece of gray brain matter oozed from a hole over his ear—and yet, only look! He sat his saddle! And thanks to the crowning touch added by Two Twists, a hunk of half-eaten venison protruded from his mouth!

A hideous shriek of terror was taken up by many others. Braves ran fleeing toward the far end of camp. In the ensuing confusion, the two

Cheyennes slipped quickly down into the corral and cut out four strong ponies.

"Brothers!" Little Horse greeted them back at the hidden copse, relief evident in his voice. "It sounds as if they have all lost their wits! We were sure you were both dead and the Wendigo was working his way around to us!"

"I paused to pluck these from their camp," Touch the Sky said with casual bravado, handing Little Horse the Medicine Arrows as if they were a mere afterthought. "Now tuck those away safely and prepare to ride, warrior. We still have a fight ahead with the sentries on that slope!"

"Cheyenne Headmen! You know why we have been called into special council. Arrow Keeper has left us. No man knows if he is dead or alive. Until we have proof of either, his name may be spoken. But none dispute that he is gone. And now we must choose a new shaman and Keeper of the Arrows."

Chief Gray Thunder paused. It was so still in the council lodge that Touch the Sky could hear the bent-sapling frame creaking. Gray Thunder sat near the center pole, the Sacred Arrows in their coyote-fur bundle at his side. He had been entrusted with their care since the joyous moment when Touch the Sky's band had ridden into camp.

"We have heard words spoken for and against Touch the Sky. We have heard words spoken for and against Medicine Flute. We have heard all the old accusations hurled between Touch the Sky and Wolf Who Hunts Smiling, along with some new ones as each proves how he out-hates the other.

"I am weary of it. The red men have enough enemies without, we need not war within. Now, all who have earned the right to speak have done so. It is time to give over with words and let the stones speak."

Touch the Sky sat in the portion of the council lodge reserved for warriors who could speak but not yet vote. The voting Headmen filled the other part. It had been a bitter council. It was as if the departure of Arrow Keeper had signaled a new era in tribal history, an era doomed to be marked by divisive factional loyalties and a fierce struggle for control of tribal destiny.

Gray Thunder passed a rawhide pouch among the Headmen. Each of the Councillors possessed a white moonstone and a black agate. Those voting for Touch the Sky placed a white stone inside the pouch; a black stone indicated a preference for Medicine Flute.

For a moment, as the pouch was finally handed back to Gray Thunder, Touch the Sky met the eyes of Wolf Who Hunts Smiling. Both braves were equally apprehensive. Each knew that this vote today meant more than just a new shaman. It would shape the very mission and destiny of the tribe.

Touch the Sky's gut tensed as he watched his chief open the pouch and hold it over the robe underneath him, preparing to spill out the contents. Again the young brave felt the weight of his loneliness as he wished, yet again, that Arrow Keeper could still be here.

Gray Thunder spilled out the stones, counted them into two piles. Then he nodded as if inwardly satisfied that justice had been done.

He looked up at the others.

"The stones have spoken," he announced. "And this place hears me when I say the tribe has spoken with one voice. From this day forth, Cheyenne law and title are clear. Touch the Sky is our new shaman and Keeper of the Arrows!"

Little Horse, Two Twists, and Tangle Hair—still walking with a hickory cane—rose as one, raising a mighty shout of triumph and support. Other members of the Bow String Soldier troop also cheered, as did various admirers of the tall Cheyenne.

But clearly Touch the Sky's enemies had been ready for this moment. And Chief Gray Thunder's conciliatory words about speaking in one voice had been wasted on them. the division in the tribe's future power struggle was made clear when, to the last man, the Bull Whip troopers stood up and silently walked out, following their leader, Lone Bear.

Every Cheyenne remaining in the lodge knew there could be no stronger gesture of contempt for the proceedings short of taking over the village by raw power. For the protestors had walked out without the final prayer or smoking to the

Four Directions. In effect, they were saying the council never took place and would not be recognized.

"Congratulations, brother," Little Horse told him later that morning. "Arrow Keeper picked you out long ago to be our medicine man. Now his choice finally has the sanction of council on it."

Touch the Sky nodded. He had just finished moving his tipi to the empty hummock where Arrow Keeper's had once stood—the custom when a new shaman took over. But he nodded across the central camp clearing. Black Elk and Wolf Who Hunts Smiling stood in the doorway of the Bull Whip lodge, watching him. Medicine Flute slouched there, too, bone flute dangling from his mouth.

"It has the sanction of council, truly. But the elders voted out of respect for Arrow Keeper's wishes, not out of love for me. Not only is Sis-ki-dee still out there somewhere, plotting more schemes from the black heart of his sickness, but my enemies right here still dream of stringing their new bows with my guts."

"Let them dream," Little Horse scoffed. "The man who uses your gut for bowstring would have a long-flying arrow indeed."

"I would rather have my gut."

Still, his friend's words rallied the troubled Touch the Sky. He glanced at Black Elk's tipi and again heard Arrow Keeper's words: *There will be trouble ahead for you, trouble behind for Honey Eater.*

Then let the fight come, he vowed. For her sake, he was ready. A man might quickly tire of struggling for his own life but for Honey Eater he would die a thousand times and call those deaths better than one long life without her.

Touch the Sky looked at his friend. "Let us go work our ponies, brother. The next fight is coming, and we have been promised a share in it."

Little Horse grinned at this show of spirit. But then, he had come to expect such mettle from this tall brave who was marked out for trouble.

"As you say, shaman."